Redeemer Chronicles 2:
The Holy War

By Julie C. Gilbert

Love Science Fiction or Mystery?

Choose your adventure!

Visit: http://www.juliecgilbert.com/

Dedication:

To all those who enjoyed Awakening and wanted Vic's journey to continue. Thank you for the encouragement.

Special Thanks:
To Rachel Rossano for a lovely cover.

Table of Contents:

Who's Who and What's What

Aeris – a planet created by Kailon

People Types:
Saroth – A people who live on the east side of Aeris's main continent. They are usually Gifted in the darker four of the seven magic schools and tend to become Destroyers, Shapeshifters, Conjurers, or Minders.
Arkonai – A people who live mainly in the northwest corner of Aeris's main continent. They are usually Gifted in the lighter three of the seven magic schools. Most Arkonai with access to magic become Seekers, Guardians, or Healers.
Bereft – Majority of people on Aeris who have no access to magic.

Other:
Victoria Saveron (Vic) – The Chosen Redeemer; father is Arkonai; mother was Saroth
The Lady – immortal servant of Kailon
Kailon – the Eternal King
The Dark Man (the Outcast) – immortal who led a rebellion against Kailon

Bereft:
Sara Andari – native of Coldhaven; devoted follower of Kailon and his servant, The Lady
Ederon – native of Coldhaven; captive
Willow Ezard – native of New Haven
Ryle Ezard – native of New Haven; Willow's son

Arkonai:
Daniel Saveron – Vic's father; huntsman; Seeker
Tellen – Vic's friend; Guardian
Jordan Lekros – Supreme Huntmaster
Devin (Shadow) – son of Supreme Huntmaster Jordan Lekros; Seeker; Gatekeeper
Dina – daughter of Supreme Huntmaster Jordan Lekros; Seeker
Galeric – Huntmaster; Resolute commander of a mixed Arkonai and Bereft army

Saroth:

Jackson Castaloni – Vic's uncle; servant of the Outcast; Conjurer
Alec Castaloni – Vic's cousin; Jackson's ward; Minder
Katrina Polani – Vic's friend; Shapeshifter
Marcus Polani – Katrina's father; Spymaster; Minder
Adam Castillo – servant of the Lady; Katrina's twin brother; Shapeshifter

What's Gone on Before?

Contains spoilers if you haven't read Awakening.

In *Redeemer Chronicles 1: Awakening* Victoria Saveron begins her journey as the Chosen Redeemer. Her quest to find her father quickly turns dangerous when the people of Coldhaven trade Vic, Katrina, and Tellen for the lives of two kidnapped villagers. She's taken to Fort Amareth where her uncle forces her to open a Darkland portal. Vic can open portals to many worlds, including Kailon's homeland. Now that the first battle is over, Vic and her companions must choose what to do next. Only one thing is certain: war is coming to Aeris.

Chapter 1:
Gatekeepers

Victoria Saveron
Courtyard Ruins, Fort Amareth

I spend a couple of hours lying on my back next to my father until he rises—despite much protesting from everybody—and leaves to help make a camp out of nothing. The younger huntsmen, Tellen and Shadow, easily accept orders from my father. Daniel Saveron may wear the lowly rank of an ordinary huntsman because of his differences with the Arkonai High Council, but he commands respect by the way he carries himself. Even recovering from a recent mortal wound doesn't slow him down much. I try not to think about miraculously snatching him back from the Veil's gates so recently, but I can't stop the endless parade of events charging through my mind.

The last few days are among my least favorite ever. I guess it started when my father went on a hunt to fulfill a contract, leaving me with my two friends, Tellen and Katrina. Zombies forced us to flee my home, so we went to Coldhaven. There, the situation went from bad to worse when the villagers decided to ransom us to Huntsman Oren for some of their own. I'll have to ask Katrina and Tellen how they escaped. Last I saw them, they were being led away by one of Oren's men and a bunch of village militiamen.

My feet ache with the memory of the long journey to Fort Amareth, and my heart aches with the memory of what we found here. Supreme Huntmaster Jordan Lekros had hired Oren at the behest of my own uncle, Jackson Castaloni. I still cannot fathom what possessed those two to work together. They claim it was to draw out my father to gain my bracers, but what good would the magic bracers do them?

Forcing those thoughts aside, I let other questions come to the surface in my mind.

How did my father get here?

Though I'll admit my grasp on the local geography is sketchy, I don't think there's a traveler's portal near here. Come to think of it, Father has always shown up whenever I faced true peril. Not that that's happened too many times in my thirteen years of life. I add the fact to the mountain of mysteries my father needs to explain someday.

What happens now?

I don't have much time to ponder answers to that one.

Done with her camp setup duties, Katrina comes over to me, shapeshifts into a dog, and settles down next to me, pinning my left arm in place. I'm about to question her when Sara Andari comes over to explain.

"Let her comfort ya, lass. She'll at least keep ya warm until the lads can build a proper fire. There's not much in the way of good brush hereabouts." The Coldhaven girl kneels beside me and holds up a waterbag. "Here now, take a drink and rest."

After weighing the cost of arguing with her, I submit to a short drink from the waterbag. The cool water and the solid warmth of Katrina's dog form both lift my spirits. My left arm begins to tingle. I shift enough to relieve the pressure. Sara tries to get me to take a second drink, but I weakly shake my head and try to distract her with conversation.

"What about the vines?" I ask, referring to the massive vines covering nearly every surface of the fort's crumbling walls. A dull pain creeps through my head, but I try to ignore it.

"There's a curse on this place," Sara says, sounding oddly cheery. "I believe burning any part of those evil vines would go ill for us, but don't worry, young Victoria. We'll have a proper camp in no time. Yer da will see to that. Meanwhile, Master Adam will guard us until they return."

It takes my mind a second to translate the word "da" and know she's referring to my father. In response, I try to lift my head enough to look around. I catch sight of the large, beautiful gray wolf trotting back and forth across the walls surrounding the courtyard. He leaps gracefully from broken places back to sturdy stones, maintaining a steady vigil.

"Yer da's gone with the Arkonai lads to get supplies from Coolwater Creek," Sara explains, correctly reading my need to see him.

"He'll be back soon."

"He's going on foot?" I question, simply hoping I make enough sense to be understood. It took us hours to get here on horses. I can't imagine how long it would take to walk the distance. "How?"

"That Shadow fellow's a most unusual Seeker," Sara says with quiet awe. She shifts to a more comfortable position and settles the waterbag on her lap before finishing the announcement. "He's a Gatekeeper."

I draw a surprised breath. Blessed by the Lady, Gatekeepers have the power to create new, if temporary, portals that allow quick travel between many places on this world. The traveler's portals connecting key locations are said to be left by the Gatekeepers of old. I'd always believed they disappeared from Aeris around the time the Redeemers faded into history several centuries ago. Nothing should surprise me anymore. I suppose it's no more shocking than the notion that I'm the Chosen Redeemer. If rumors and legends can be trusted, that means I'm destined to see a whole lot more of the impossible. The thought of the Gatekeepers' return causes hope to fill my chest, nearly bringing me to tears.

They are another sign. The end of the dark times draws near, and Kailon willing, I will be a part of it. I don't know how, but I finally believe I will know when I need to know. The phrase holds much more power than the many times my father's uttered it to put off explaining something.

"He's an abomination," calls a bitter male voice, pulling me from my thoughts. "They all are, especially that Gatekeeper."

Twisting my head around to the right, I barely glimpse a trussed up man leaning against the wall leading into the fort proper. I return my head to a resting position once I'm certain the man's no threat to me. Keeping it that way would only worsen my headache. The man looks familiar, but I can't really place him.

"How can ye say such things, Ederon?" asks Sara. "The world has not been blessed with a Gatekeeper in many years. How can ye not draw hope from such good fortune?"

"Good fortune," the man repeats softly. He mostly sounds weary now. He's one of Oren's men, but he's no Arkonai. He's a Bereft from Coldhaven, like Sara. "Don't you understand what the arrival of a Gatekeeper means?" He lets only a second pass before making his revelation. "It means war."

Sara's soft hand finds mine and picks it up. Once again, I'm amazed she can stand the cold, clammy feeling of the dead flesh there. I'm not sure where my leather gloves have gone. Huntmaster Oren had Tellen remove them before binding my wrists when he first captured us. I've not seen them since, but at least the sight of my right hand has ceased to bother me.

"Aye. But war would come either way," says Sara. "It's been coming for ages since the rise in the number of Darkland creatures."

"They caused this!" Ederon shouts. The pain in his voice tells me there's more to him and his story than I understand. "We should drive the magic ones from the land. They don't belong here."

"None of us do," Sara replies. "Not one of us deserves a blessed day of life. That we can even draw a breath of air is a miracle worth our wondering or at the very least our appreciation."

Her voice shifts to that ageless, melodious voice I've come to associate with the Lady.

"War is terrible, but it will cleanse the land of evil."

I'm not certain whom Sara's addressing, but Ederon grunts with disgust and falls silent. Sara sits beside me gently holding my hand for another few moments before shaking her shoulders and squeezing my hand.

"Oy, look at me sitting here like I've not a care in the world." Placing my hand across my stomach, Sara rolls to a kneeling position again. "'Tis high time I make good use of me legs and get some chores done." She pats my right shoulder. "Give a shout if ya need me, lass. I'll not be going far. A place like this ought to have something useful. Perhaps I'll find us a cooking pot so we can have a good meal when yer da returns with supplies."

I want to tell her not to leave, but she's probably right. There's much to be done. I try to rise, but Sara holds me in place with two fingers.

"None of that, dear one. You've done more than enough for the day. Let others care for ya while ya can. A time will come when much will be required of ya, Victoria. Until then, let us do our part." Leaning forward, Sara places a soft kiss on my forehead and adjusts the cloak someone's placed under my head for a pillow.

Katrina's fallen asleep beside me. Her even breathing soothes me.

The courtyard shadows lengthen, and I doze off and let questions bounce around my head.

Where should we go?

I'm fairly certain I'll find out soon enough and that I won't like the answer either way.

If Shadow's a Gatekeeper, are there others?

Instinct tells me there must be. If that's true, we must find them soon. When war truly breaks out, Gatekeepers will mean the difference between victory and defeat. Whichever side can command the most portals can move spies, troops, supplies, and the terrible instruments of war quickly from place to place. Depending on the number and skill of those Gatekeepers, they could sack whole cities with a handful of fighters. Traveler's portals exist already, but Gatekeepers can create new ones. It exhausts them, but properly supported, they can turn the tide of any battle. I've read at least three books that discuss the impact of Gatekeepers upon the Great Wars of the past. If another one is coming, we'll need them.

Katrina stirs beside me. I consider waking her so we can catch up, but I'm enjoying the warmth too much. She could probably hold the conversation in her dog form, but that would be too strange. I need normal right now. I want to forget that we just fought with a fabled army of white-robed warriors from another world against a horde of zombies.

I don't know what my Uncle Jack's up to, but it can't be good. My brief encounter with him convinces me he's crazy for power, but what is he trying to accomplish? He forced me to open a Darkland portal, but what does opening those accomplish?

How does the Supreme Huntmaster fit in?

The Arkonai have never been overly fond of the Saroth. That's part of my father's trouble with his people. They outright rejected his decision to marry my mother. I suddenly experience a sensation of loss. Next instant, I'm weeping, and I don't know why. It's not from missing my mother. In truth, I hardly knew her before she died in the same attack that left me needing the magic bracers to keep from changing into a zombie.

The Lady's voice fills my mind.

"Do not fight the pain, Victoria. I'm sorry you must experience this. What you feel is a remnant of the loss Kailon felt when the Outcast defiled Aeris with Darkland creatures. This is the wrong you will help me right if you are willing."

Doubts still crowd my mind, but now that I'm in this fight, I want to finish it.

Chapter 2:
Two Paths to War

The Lady
Central War Room, Fort Medron

"I should be king already," Jackson Castaloni mutters. He's been pacing around the room for about half an hour, filling the air with complaints and breathing threats against my Chosen Redeemer. In and around these, he murmurs the phrases of a summoning ritual.

I'm afraid that if nothing happens soon, young Alec Castaloni will lose interest and wander away from his post. Unlike the last time I visited Fort Medron—when Jackson had Alec help during the ritual that summoned three Denkari from the Darklands—this time, he specifically forbade Alec from attending the meeting. Thankfully, Jackson's frequent absences from the fort have given Alec much time to explore the empty rooms and abandoned hallways. The boy peers down into the room through a small crack in ceiling just above the east wall.

The room shimmers and a hole appears in the Veil, allowing a figure wearing dark robes with the cowl raised to step through and stand next to Jackson.

"To be king, you must first create a throne," says the figure in a low, masculine voice. The man crosses his arms in a casual pose. The hood prevents me from seeing his face, and his presence feels tainted with evil. "Do not fear. Your mission was largely successful."

"We lost. Victoria's alive, and I don't have the bracers," Jackson summarizes. "How is that a success?"

"We've barely begun to fight, and you now have me," says the figure, sounding amused. The man shrugs. "The magic bracers would

6

speed my return to full power, but I have other means of gaining strength. You are not my only servant, nor my only plan, though you will be my first choice for king once this tiny, troublesome world is brought to heel."

"Why do you care about our fate if we're just a 'tiny, troublesome world'?" Jackson wonders.

"For reasons I cannot fathom, my enemy delights in the people here. Therefore, I will deprive him of them one by one," replies the figure. This must be the Dark Man, the Outcast's physical manifestation. "You can have the world when his servants are my slaves. To that end, we have a lot of work to do."

"What do you require of me?" Jackson asks formally.

"Chaos," says the Dark Man. "You will create a war to end all wars. The more trouble that reigns, the easier it will be to summon an army capable of conquering everybody who resists."

"And how shall I create this war?" Jackson inquires. He sounds almost bored with the idea.

"Use your contacts. Send emissaries to every corner of the continent. The time has come to take the fight to the Arkonai and the Bereft alike. The Saroth are my chosen people, but before you can have peace, you must destroy the inferior beings polluting the land with their presence."

Jackson appears stunned by the enormity of the task set before him.

"Where shall I start, my lord?"

"I have servants already building you a proper army in the Badlands and the Ashlands, but you must gather every capable Conjurer to move them as needed," explains the Dark Man. "Bribe them, threaten them, hold their loved ones hostage. I don't care what means you use, only secure their oaths of cooperation and make sure the contracts are binding."

Jackson nods at the order, appearing a tad more comfortable now that he has a plan to follow. He's done work like this before to secure his inheritance of the Castaloni lands and businesses, destroying Victoria's mother in the process. It is a familiar tactic to him.

"And bring me the Chosen Redeemer," orders the Dark Man. "You will need me to deal with her."

"She's just a girl," Jackson says.

The Dark Man's voice hardens at Jackson's casual dismissal.

"She represents hope. That is the one thing we cannot abide."

The Dark Man's clothes flicker. "My time is short so I will be brief. Know that I am working to stir the Arkonai and the Bereft to war too. They will have weapons that can harm you. Tread with care. Spread rumors and lies. Exaggerate death tolls. Feed misinformation. Wherever you can sow discord, do so. The Tariku League could be a great asset or a stumbling block. See to it they join us. I will send you more thoughts on these matters when I can, but get started soon."

My spirits sink, but I maintain enough presence to prevent Alec from revealing himself. Adam will have much work to do. I will send him to the Bereft to continue warning them against lies. Keeping Victoria safe will be much harder now. The schemes of men are one thing, but with the Outcast involving himself, the chances of maintaining peace just grew much thinner.

After sending Alec to his room, I withdraw to check on the Arkonai leaders. They are holding a meeting that will determine much. I need to know how successful the Outcast's initial schemes are if I'm to know how to best direct my peacekeepers.

***

The Lady
Deliverance Hall, City of Bastion
Throughout the ages, I have been to Deliverance Hall many times, but today, the atmosphere feels different. There has always been a deep sense of history and gravity due to the weighty matters considered here. I feel none of that. Fear, anger, and mistrust dominate every feature I see. Most are familiar faces: Lady Callista of Aridel, Lord Gannon Vek of Castleton, Huntmaster Lamir of Bastion, Huntmaster Callen of Cardeth, and, of course, Supreme Huntmaster Jordan Lekros. The half-dozen others are new to me, but I do not have time to familiarize myself with their minds. The debate must be old at this point for emotions to be in such a fine twist.

"The Resolute are a danger to everybody," declares Huntmaster Callen. The fine fabric of his forest green robes tells me his family's many farms must be doing well. "We must control them soon." He resists the urge to pound the sturdy wooden table each member of the Arkonai High Council is arrayed around. Nevertheless, his fists are tight with conviction.

"At least they're doing something to combat the numerous zombie outbreaks," Lady Callista says. Contrary to convention, she wears many rows of thin gold chains around her neck and displays long, sparkling jewels from her ears. The soft look of her hands tells me it's been many years since her hands have actually touched a bow. "All we seem to accomplish is talking ourselves in circles."

"Have you listened to their rhetoric?" demands Huntmaster Callen. "They're blaming the outbreaks on the Saroth."

"Don't you need a Conjurer to summon zombies?" asks one of the Arkonai whom I do not recognize. The sound of his voice gives me the opening to discover his name and home city. He is Lord Asalor Ravine of Urdik.

"No," Huntmaster Callen says. "A strong enough Seeker or Minder can bind them to a scroll. One need not be a Conjurer, but that's not the point!"

"What is your point?" asks the Supreme Huntmaster. Jordan Lekros leans forward, indicating his interest in Callen's answer.

"With our huntsmen spread thin and the cries for aid on the rise, this is not the time to be provoking the Saroth," explains Huntmaster Callen. The cadence of his speech speaks of his impatience with his colleagues. "Like it or not, we may need to work with them to drive back these abominations."

His last statement causes an uproar. Roughly half the Arkonai leaders agree with him and the others dissent—loudly. For several moments, nobody can understand anything above the din. At last, the Supreme Huntmaster bangs a gavel on the wooden table to restore order. Reluctantly, the others heed the call and look to their chief.

Jordan stands, drawing their eyes upward.

"We should join them." His announcement stuns the room into stillness and silence.

"You ... can't be serious." Huntmaster Callen's the first to recover. "They stand for everything we're not."

"They want to fight the Darkland creatures. That's good enough for me," declares Lady Callista. "Supreme Huntmaster, my huntsmen are at your disposal."

Two of the other leaders also pledge their support.

"The Resolute will fall into line if we show our strength," says the Supreme Huntmaster.

"I cannot ... and I will not pledge my people to follow madmen." Huntmaster Callen's voice starts out low but quickly strengthens with his resolve. His brown eyes sweep over his peers, pleading for their attention. "They're advocating for the slaughter or enslavement of every Saroth. Such blind hatred will destroy us, even if we survive the Darkland invasion."

Most of the other council members agree with him.

"What are you proposing?" inquires Lord Gannon Vek. He pitches the words lightly, but his steely gray eyes demand answers.

"Let us send ambassadors to the Saroth," says Huntmaster Callen. "If we denounce the Resolute and distance ourselves from their abhorrent teachings, we can form a treaty with the Saroth. If we do not actively pursue peace with them, we risk a war on two fronts."

"You would have us join with evil to fight it?" wonders Lady Callista.

"They're not evil!" Huntmaster Callen's frustration rings through his protest.

Raising both hands, Jordan Lekros waits for the mutterings to subside again.

"Friends. Fellow huntsmen. Brothers—and dear sister—let us agree on a few facts," the Supreme Huntmaster begins reasonably. He smiles broadly and sends a friendly smile Lady Callista's way. "Every one of us wishes to protect our people and the Bereft."

Everybody nods agreement.

"The time has come for each of us to look to our own houses. If we cannot protect what is precious to us, we are nothing." Jordan stops speaking to let the words sink deep into his listeners. "I believe it's time to declare Nerulic Victis against the Darkland invaders. Our brothers and sisters—the Resolute—have already done this. Even now, Galeric raises an army of Bereft to battle our enemies. It's time we too gather our forces and take the fight to the enemy. If the Saroth stand with us, fine. If not, we will sweep them aside with the Darkland creatures."

Once again, the Supreme Huntmaster manages to cause a complete and utter silence. His speech hangs in the air like a cloud of doom. Even those who support the idea look grim. Nerulic Victis—literally "no rest until victory"—is a holy war the likes of which the Arkonai people have not declared for centuries.

"Will you order it, sir?" Huntmaster Callen asks hoarsely. The strain on his face tells me this is causing him a crisis of conscience.

Every eye swings back to the Supreme Huntmaster. I feel the frantic calculations running through Jordan's head. If he orders it, the High Council will be forced to vote immediately. It's a gamble. Should the vote go his way, the entirety of the Arkonai people would be his to command until the holy war ends. Should the vote fail, he would lose much more than the bid. He'd have to resign as Supreme Huntmaster.

If he lets each follow their conscience, he'll gain some support but certainly not all. Jordan Lekros has always been a cautious leader. Thus, his next words do not surprise me.

"No, I will not order it. This is a matter of conscience," the Supreme Huntmaster says. "Return to your homes and make your own decisions. I have declared my path and would welcome any of you who would stand with me against the coming darkness. Should the Lady's grace rest upon us we will obtain victory quickly."

Hearing my name used thus is painful. He's practically called those who fail to stand with him cowards. In a culture deeply steeped in honor and tradition, it's a powerful insult.

Having had his say, Jordan closes the meeting and exits. One by one, the others collect their entourages from the waiting area and slip back through the traveler's portals to their own cities. Finally, only Huntmaster Lamir—the host—and Huntmaster Callen remain.

Callen has not moved from his seat. He wears a bleak expression and holds his head with both hands, making a mess of his normally neat graying brown hair.

"What will you do, my friend?" Lamir keeps his tone gentle.

The question drives the despair from Callen's eyes. Determination quickly takes its place.

"I will do what I proposed. I'll send an envoy to the Saroth requesting a formal treaty of non-aggression and mutual aid to fight the Darkland creatures."

Lamir waits a second for Callen to continue before asking the obvious question.

"Who will you send?"

"My son," Callen answers. "Tellen will know the right words to say. He's already traveling with Daniel Saveron's girl and the daughter of Marcus Polani. The Polani girl should be able to get him an audience with the Tariku League as I believe her father works for the Council." He silently considers the plan. Now that I can focus on him, I feel his fear for his son. This will not be an easy mission. If the wrong people find out Tellen's even going to attempt such peace talks, they'll kill him. "What will you do?" Callen asks the question to remove the focus from his fears.

"Warn young Shadow," Lamir answers gravely.

Those three words send a jolt through me. I dive deeper into Lamir's mind to see what he fears. When I find it, I understand. After promising to carry the message to Shadow, I leave the city of Bastion altogether and seek out Victoria and her companions.

Chapter 3:
Separate Missions

Katrina Polani
Temporary Camp, Fort Amareth

The morning dawns misty and cool. We agreed to split the night into even watches and let Vic's father make the assignments. I was given the last shift. Ours is likely the strangest camp formed in decades. We are three Arkonai huntsmen, two Saroth Shapeshifters, two ordinary Bereft, and the Chosen Redeemer encamped in the ruins of Fort Amareth. I spent most of my watch in beetle form because it's the least affected by cold temperatures, but I changed back to my human form to watch the sunrise.

In his wolf form, my brother Adam leaps onto a ruined section then jumps up again to the wall where I'm perched and sits beside me. I expect him to take on his human form and deliver the message I see burning in his eyes. Instead, he only stares at me with his pale blue eyes. A faint whine comes from his throat. He stands and gently presses his large head into my right side. I turn, and he backs up a step and releases a longer, more plaintive whine. His eyes hold sadness now. After meeting my eyes, Adam nods toward the camp below us. Then, bowing deeply, he lifts his head, yips once, and leaps off the wall, sprinting for Bleakwood Forest.

"Katrina, come eat something." The tension in Tellen's tone sets me on edge. "There's going to be a meeting afterward."

Changing to beetle form, I fly down to the camp's center where I'm met by more grim expressions. When I'm a safe distance off the ground, I initiate the change to human form and sweep my gaze over everybody, trying to decide whom to question. Vic would normally be my first choice since the girl's incapable of keeping secrets, but right now, she looks like she's fighting tears. Her father's expression is thoughtful and unreadable. Shadow's stiffness tells me he's upset, but he cloaks himself in Arkonai aloofness. I'm not likely to get any response from him. Even Sara and Ederon look subdued.

I hate being the last to know something.

Tellen hands me a bowl of stew. Fighting the petty urge to shove it back at him, I lower myself to the ground and set it carefully beside me. I also note that everybody else's food appears untouched.

"Who's going to tell me what's wrong?" I ask. I want to ask where my brother's going, but I sense that's not the heart of what troubles this group.

"They're leaving." The whispered words overwhelm Vic.

I wait for a more elaborate answer.

Ederon avoids my gaze. Sara goes to Vic and wraps our young friend in a comforting embrace. This move lowers Vic's defenses and sets the girl to quietly weeping. Tellen, Shadow, and Daniel Saveron exchange glances and subtle signals. Finally, Tellen breaks the silence.

"I received a message from my father this morning, and Sara—" Tellen stops speaking and gestures to the young woman from Coldhaven.

"The Blessed Lady showed me a dream in the wee hours," Sara explains. "She showed me pieces of the meeting that took place."

"What meeting?" I wonder. I'm not sure how Arkonai mental communication works, but I suppose it's not far-fetched to believe that their Seekers have similar gifts to Minders. I'm starting to believe Daniel Saveron's claim that the distinction of magic schools is a human convenience. The Gifts simply exist, manifesting in accordance with the nature of the one who accesses the magic. That would explain Tellen's ability to cast lightning while not sharing any other Destroyer traits.

"The Arkonai High Council," Shadow answers. His expression displays his agitation. "My father has declared a holy war and effectively joined a small but powerful cult that calls itself the Resolute."

I'm not picking up on why a holy war would be bad. On the surface, it sounds like something that could rally the Arkonai into fighting the Darkland creatures. That part would be good, but the three huntsmen before me look troubled.

"The Resolute have been around for many years, and they are fierce fighters," Vic's father admits, "but they're also fanatics who hold deep convictions about the purity and supremacy of the Arkonai people."

"That makes them our enemy," Tellen declares. The anger in his tone seems disproportionate to Daniel's words.

I cast a curious glance at my friend.

"Were we at their mercy, none of us would survive," Shadow explains. A bitter smile moves the mask the young man always wears. "Except maybe me, for my father's sake, at least until they know my heart." By the end, I doubt Shadow's actually talking to the rest of us.

"You, they'd kill because you're Saroth," Vic's father explains. "Me, they'd kill because I married a Saroth. Vic, they'd kill—"

"Because of her mother," I finish, finally understanding their concern. "So, what does this mean for us?" We need to leave this place, but Vic's earlier words tell me decisions have already been made. We're likely not leaving for the same destination.

"We need to separate," says Shadow.

"No! Please!" Vic begs, choking on her tears.

"Shhhhh. Settle down, lass," Sara urges. "We only mean to keep ya safe."

Vic's grief flips to anger, but she's too upset for more words, which I think is for the best.

Daniel Saveron explains for my benefit.

"I need to leave."

I raise an eyebrow. I'm not impressed by the ability of Arkonai huntsmen to clarify matters.

"I'm under contract, which means the High Council could use another Seeker to find me. With my contract incomplete, I'm a danger to the group." He meets my gaze. "If the purists gain control of the Council, they may search for us. I will not allow them to find my daughter through me."

"That's why we're leaving."

Shadow's statement confuses me.

"I understand why he needs to leave, but why you?" I ask Shadow.

"With my aid he can finish his contract quickly, and I need his help with a private matter. Then, if the Lady wills it, we will meet the rest of you at the Alamon Temple."

Quelling the urge to pry, I nod. Being neutral ground, the

temple makes a logical choice for our destination.

"Why don't we go to Bastion?" I wonder. "There's probably a portal to Temperance, if not the temple itself. That's neutral ground too. A journey on foot will take us weeks."

"There are too many Arkonai in Bastion," Tellen points out. "From what my father says, it sounds like the Resolute control the Council. You wouldn't be safe."

I'm about to inquire why they don't just send me with Vic's father when he speaks.

"The journey will keep the rest of you on the move," Daniel explains. "When Shadow and I complete our separate missions, we'll find you and escort you the rest of the way to the Alamon Temple."

"There's a traveler's portal in Coolwater Creek that will take us to Newhaven," says Tellen. "From there, we can take a different portal to Midpoint. If we can barter for horses there, it should only be another few days to the temple."

"Why are we going to the temple and not Temperance?" I inquire. An instinct I cannot define makes me wary. "What is our destination beyond the temple?"

"We need you to get us into Caramore," Tellen says. "My father has charged me with arranging a treaty between our people, at least until the Darkland crisis is over, and your people can keep Vic safe."

"Vic's uncle tried to kill her," I note. I'm not certain how I feel about the request. My people are extremely reclusive. A truce seems like a good idea, but the opposition to a declaration of peace will be fierce from both sides. "The Castaloni family is very powerful in Caramore. Are you sure you wish to go there?"

"No, but what choice do we have?" Tellen asks. "What are the chances members of the Tariku League will answer an invitation to come to a peace summit in Cardeth?"

"None," I admit. "But do you realize what you're asking?" My stomach flutters. "If they don't like what you say, they'll kill you."

"Then I hope they like what I say." Tellen attempts a smile for my sake.

"I doubt they'd kill ya with a witness." Sara's words slice through the grim silence that falls over us. "I'll be going with ya anyways, and that's that."

Several of us open our mouths to protest, but Sara's fierce look stops us.

"If ya let me do the talking, I can help ya blend in on our travels. Besides, this one will need care, and I'll do enough praying to make the undead want to turn back around and head home."

I don't doubt her words or her logic, but without magic to defend her, Sara's chances of surviving the trip are not favorable.

"What about him?" I ask, nodding to Ederon.

"We'll take him to Coolwater Creek and turn him over to the village elders," says Vic's father. "They'll probably return him to Coldhaven."

It's a kinder fate than the man deserves, but with the number of crises facing us, we can't waste time prosecuting a man who found himself on the wrong end of a dark deal.

"You should give up. You'll never make it." Ederon's tone lacks malice.

"Do not say such things, Ederon," Sara scolds. "After what we saw yesterday, how can ye still not believe?"

"I saw the same signs you do, Sara," says Ederon. "I just believe in a different solution. Forgive me if I cannot put my faith in a weeping child. When I'm free, I'll be turning my sword on the Darkland spawn. Make no mistake about that."

Ederon's unexpected speech eases each of us into our own thoughts. I don't feel like eating, but I force the stew down anyway. We will need every scrap of strength for what lies ahead.

Chapter 4:
Official Contracts

Victoria Saveron
Temporary Camp, Fort Amareth

"Is this really necessary?" I direct the question to my father, but he, Tellen, and Shadow each nod once in that infuriating Arkonai manner that tells me they're merely being polite in asking. Regardless of what I say, they'll do what they please and claim it's for my own good.

Having spent more than my fair share of tears this morning, I move into the exasperated phase. The Saroth half of me is thoroughly annoyed with the Arkonai and their obsession with contracts. They want to write two official Guardian contracts, one for me and one for my father. Once completed, the contracts would bind Tellen to my service and Shadow to Father. Because my father is in his overprotective mode, he also wants to write a secondary contract to hire Shadow as my backup guardian should Tellen require the aid. Who knew Seekers could even offer Guardian contracts?

In truth, I know trouble lies ahead, but I don't see how official contracts will change the situation much. After our recent adventures here in Fort Amareth, I probably couldn't get rid of Tellen if I wanted to. The same goes for Katrina and Sara. Thank goodness the Saroth and the Bereft are much more normal about notions of friendship and loyalty.

A long moment passes while I stare at the men arrayed before me. They stare back expectantly. I blink, unsure of what they're waiting for.

"It's your move, Vic," says Shadow. A slow smile crosses his face, moving the black mask he always wears. "We need your permission to proceed."

I consider making him remove his mask to gain my permission but the grave look in my father's eyes demands I take this seriously.

"You have it," I assure them. "What do you need me to do?"

Looking relieved, my father comes over to my makeshift bed of straw and grass with a blanket thrown over it and lifts me to my feet. My legs feel unsteady, but I can stand if I lean heavily upon my father.

"Hold out your right hand, Vic," Father instructs. "Palm up."

As I follow the direction, Tellen and Shadow make almost identical waving gestures. The air next to them splits apart, and three scrolls fly out of the Veil and into their outstretched hands. Tellen catches one and Shadow catches two. At another gesture, Shadow's second scroll leaves his hand and hovers obediently near his right shoulder. A quill and ink set appears before the small tear in the Veil mends itself. I'm not sure who's controlling it, but the quill dips itself into the ink, shakes off the excess, and settles on my palm.

Holding the scrolls over their hearts, Tellen and Shadow close their eyes and bow their heads. I'm too fascinated to think the behavior strange, and somehow, I understand that they're putting the final touches on their contracts. I've never given much thought to huntsmen and their contracts before. Although there are females who choose that life, I knew from an early age that having a Saroth mother meant I could not join the Arkonai Hunting Guild.

Tellen finishes first. Stepping forward, he drops to a knee before me and unfurls the scroll near the bottom where I see two lines with x's next to them. One line already bears Tellen's signature. The other line awaits my signature. The page is filled with tight, neat script in Arphese, an older, very formal version of the modern language used by the Arkonai people. I don't know enough of the language to understand, but I trust my friend and my father. When my quill touches the enchanted paper, the words and the meaning of the long contract come into me in an instant.

I sign the contract, and Tellen rolls it up and brings it once again to his chest.

"With this contract, I pledge to be your Guardian until my service is no longer required. Whatever trials and dangers you face, I will face, and whatever pain you must bear, I will bear. May the Lady's grace rest upon us."

The quill slips from my hand and hovers near me. Before I can pluck it from the air, my father presses a silver coin into my hand.

"Give him this and accept the contract," says my father.

I slowly place the small coin into Tellen's outstretched left hand.

"I accept this contract and your service." The weight of the pledge nearly overwhelms me. Tears spring to my eyes. I'm usually not this weepy, but to my surprise, I see unshed tears glisten in Tellen's eyes too.

He presses the coin to the scroll and sends both back into the Veil. Next, Tellen cups my damaged right hand between his solid, perfect hands and squeezes gently. After a long moment, he offers me a smile, releases my hand, climbs to his feet, and retreats to stand beside Shadow again.

The signing and accepting procedure repeats itself with Shadow. When my part is complete, Father eases me back onto the makeshift bed and goes through a similar ritual with Shadow for his own protection. I always thought Arkonai could only have one active contract at a time, but the terms in Shadow's secondary contract with me hold that should the peril facing me reach a certain threshold, his first contract for my father will be temporarily suspended. Very few Seekers can write such contracts because they'd have no way of getting to their secondary target, but Shadow's special. Come to think of it, perhaps this is how Father finds me in times of trouble.

My musings are interrupted by sudden clapping. A look left shows me Sara and Katrina, the former beaming and the latter wearing a knowing grin.

Did I miss something? Since when did contract signing become a spectator sport?

Ritual over, the men wander away to complete the preparations for their journeys. A painful pang touches me. I realize it's already mid-morning and we'll be leaving soon. Fort Amareth holds no real comfort for me, but my father is here. In my head, I sort of get his reasons for leaving me again, but the rest of me hates it. I'm glad Shadow will be with him, and that the mission should not take long to complete. Still, cold fear grips me.

Before I know it, Katrina and Sara are beside me on my right and left respectively.

"We're with you too, Vic," Katrina promises.

Their added support comforts me, but the fears in me change shape. I don't want to let them down. I don't want to let anyone down, but I also can't see a way to fulfill their blind faith in me.

"What do I do?" My whispered question contains every scrap of self-doubt I can muster. I know the basic plan. I might have been caught up in a series of fits this morning, but I heard enough to know we're supposed to go to Coolwater Creek next with Caramore being the ultimate destination. What I can't begin to wrap my mind around is what I'm supposed to do once there.

In the ensuing silence, I slip into despairing thoughts. The Saroth won't listen to me. I'm a disgrace to their pure bloodlines. They probably won't even let me speak to their ruling council. If we're lucky, they'll let Katrina tell them of the rising tides of war facing the world. Even her word may fail to move them to action, but we have to try.

Attempting to fight the Darkland invaders without the Saroth would be foolish. They're one of the only two people groups capable of accessing magic Gifts. We'll need practitioners from all seven schools of magic to win the coming war. Destroyers, Shapeshifters, and Minders can carry on the bulk of the fighting. Seekers and Guardians will be able to protect the fighters. Healers can pick up where protection fails, and Conjurers can keep the lines supplied. It sounds easy in my head. First, we have to draw the Saroth out of their safe zone.

Caramore is isolated by natural formations. The few accessible places are carefully guarded by magic portals. The World's End Mountains form the northern border. These flow into the Silver Forest which runs directly into the Kartoff Mountains. The North Castlerock River, the Castlerock Mountains, and the Enchanted Forest separate the western border of Caramore from most of the Badlands. The South Castlerock River flows down to the Seas of Hope. The land between that river and the Seas of Abundance provide for many Saroth, especially in and around the City of Outreach, but it's not technically part of Caramore due to the Last Stand Mountains.

With that much protection, my mother's people have no reason to care about what goes on beyond those borders. If the rest of the main continent falls, the undead and other Darkland creatures will find a way in, but that may not be for years. Somehow, we must convince the Saroth to care for the fate of others now.

"We'll go to my people and convince the Tariku League to help," says Katrina. She makes it sound simple. "My father knows them well."

"After that, we'll follow the Lady's leading," Sara adds. "One thing's for sure: we'll not run out of tasks for quite a while."

"I know it must be done, but what then?" I ask my friends. "What if we can't convince the Saroth to help? Where should we send the help if by some miracle we get it?"

"Those are grand questions, they are," says Sara. "And I'm certain ye will have answers when they're needed. Until then, keep the faith."

"One thing at a time, Vic." Katrina pats my right knee. "Let's get to Caramore first. Are you strong enough for the journey?"

The old me would be insulted by such a question, but after yesterday, it's a valid concern.

"I hope so," I answer. "My head hurts, but I think I can walk. Help me up and we'll find out."

Chapter 5:
New Weapons

The Lady
Home of Councilman Jelan Balewa, City of Urdik

Daniel Saveron enjoys the sense of victory as young Lekan Balewa reunites with his family. Many tears are shed by both parents while Daniel delivers a brief report on the rescue. He and Shadow ambushed the two men guarding the child in a storage facility in a rundown section of the city. Daniel would have found the boy quickly on his own, but I led him to the correct location anyway. The child had suffered enough neglect already. The thugs holding Lekan captive until his father agreed to support legislation against the Saroth barely remembered to feed the boy. Anger burns inside me every time I think of how low people will stoop to get their way.

Soon, the boy's mother, Akuna, sweeps the child off to bed and lets the men conclude the contract. Councilman Jelan pulls a small leather pouch out from a hidden pocket of his fancy robes and holds it out to Daniel.

"Thank you for saving my boy," says the councilman. His deep voice sends words out in rumbling waves. He dashes away the last traces of tears from his dark eyes.

Accepting the payment, Daniel reaches into the Veil for the contract and marks it completed. Normally, he'd store the money with the finished contract, but he senses he'll need it soon along his travels with Shadow. Instead, he ties the thin thongs to his belt.

"Would you like me to arrange for a Guardian to be

contracted?" asks Daniel.

"I've already hired more bodyguards," replies the councilman, shaking his head. He folds his arms across his broad chest and frowns at the floor. "This should not have happened. The fact that it did is not a good sign." The words are not directed to anyone in particular so nobody speaks. Recovering from his short reverie, Jelan straightens his shoulders. "I don't know what will happen now that the Resolute supporters have a majority in the People's Council. But I promise to fight them with every trick I know."

Daniel's sharp eyes take in more of the room and his host. The lanterns hanging in strategic locations are being kept low. Accessing one of his less spectacular Gifts, Daniel expands his presence and seeks out the room's past. Several areas of the room light up in his mind's eye, showing him where objects were recently removed. The councilman's robes, though fine, are wearing thin. The tall, dark-skinned man keeps twisting a single gold ring around his left middle finger, but faint marks outline where many others once sat. Coming to a decision, Daniel yanks the money pouch off his belt and holds it out to the councilman.

The man eyes the small pouch suspiciously.

"Our contract is complete," says Daniel. "Use it to protect your family."

Jelan's arms remain firmly crossed and a stubborn look settles into place on his face.

"I suspect this plot was partly to drain your resources," Daniel explains. "If you had to resign from the Council to support your family, your enemies would gain a great victory." He smiles. "I'll not be the cause of removing one of the last voices of reason from the People's Council."

Reluctantly accepting the money, the councilman nods and sets the pouch on a table that once held a collection of fine wines.

"We should leave," Shadow notes.

Before either the councilman or Daniel can react to the urgency in Shadow's tone, a fist pounds on the front door.

"Councilman Balewa, this is Sergeant Kevan of the Urdik Homeguard. Open the door or we'll break it!" shouts a man.

Concern enters the councilman's eyes.

"Go out the back," he urges.

"If there's a room big enough for a portal, I can get us out of here," Shadow offers.

Councilman Jelan shakes his head swiftly.

"Kevan's been working with the Anti-Magic League. He trained with Galeric for a time before the Resolute commander moved his forces out of Urdik. The AML develops weapons that can be used by ordinary men against Saroth, but the weapons work against your kind of magic too."

Somebody pounds on the front door again, louder this time.

"Better answer it," says Daniel.

"Councilman!" calls Kevan. "Open up immediately and surrender the Saroth sympathizers. We have a warrant for their arrest."

"I'll handle them," declares Councilman Jelan, "but you need to go. Please. I'll send a message when I can, but you must go now."

"Gentlemen, come," says Akuna Balewa from the door leading farther into the house.

Daniel Saveron rarely avoids confrontations, but I sense this is not a conflict he's ready to face. He exchanges a quick look with Shadow and follows Akuna from the room. She threads her way through darkened rooms. They reach the doorway at the back of the house, but Daniel prevents her from opening the door.

"There are six men waiting there," he informs her.

She spins and slumps against the door, looking frightened.

A surge of alarm pulses through Daniel. Before he reasons through why, he's already moving. Grabbing Akuna's right arm, he yanks her hard, spinning her toward Shadow. The younger man catches her and pushes her down behind a thick, wooden table as a muffled boom comes from outside the door. Something slams into the door and punches a small hole through it, narrowly missing Daniel. He backpedals quickly.

Shadow mutters a curse and reaches for the dagger attached to his belt.

With a sinking feeling, Daniel reaches for the Veil and finds he cannot grasp it well enough to summon his bow or sword. Five more booms sound. Daniel flattens himself on the floor and more small objects burst through the door near the latch. The door swings open, and the men sprint forward with triumphant shouts. Sensing an opening, I urge Daniel to move.

He does.

As the first man reaches the door, Daniel throws out an arm and catches the man in the throat. His opponent drops with a gurgling noise, but Daniel's already throwing a punch at the next man in line. The man dodges, and the blow glances off his shoulder. The handle of Shadow's dagger plows into the man's temple, dropping him. The next man trips over the one felled by Shadow. Daniel pushes him hard in the chest, knocking him into the two men standing behind him.

"Stop or I'll shoot!" The young man's voice quivers with nervousness.

Shadow leaps over the pile of men in the doorway, tucks into a forward roll, and sweeps the attacker's feet. The young man cries out and drops his weapon. Shadow snatches it up before it touches the ground and tucks it into his belt. Then, in a blur of motion, he punches the last foe three times in the chest and once in the stomach. Leaning over the gasping man, Shadow places his hand over his opponent's forehead and murmurs one of the power words. The man drops unconscious. Shadow strips off the man's weapons belt. He's not sure what each pouch is for, but he understands that it might be important later.

Daniel follows suit with the others before swiftly relieving each man of the strange, hand-held weapon that had destroyed the door. During his search, he finds a small metal disk in one man's pocket. It pulses with enough dark energy to give Daniel an intense headache, but he flips it up into the air and uses one of the new weapons against it. The disk shatters into several shards. Daniel's impressed by the power packed in the new weapon, but he doesn't have time to dwell on it. Now that nothing's interfering with his access to the Veil, he opens a large enough hole to store the weapons and the leather belts Shadow confiscated from the unconscious men.

I'm proud at the care Daniel and Shadow took to not kill their enemies, but I don't think that streak will last given the intensity of the rising conflicts.

"What manner of weapon is this?" asks Shadow. He's staring down at one of the strange devices cradled in his palms.

"They call them guns," answers Akuna. "There are small and large versions. Not many can afford them yet, but their power rivals any arrow or stone shot from a sling." She shudders, seeing Shadow's fascination. "Please, be careful. Accidents have killed men before."

"I like them," says Shadow.

"Most young men do," Akuna admits with a small sigh.

"We can study them later," Daniel notes. "We need to leave. Open the portal."

His keen ears have picked up the sound of running footsteps.

Shadow draws a deep breath, holds out his arms, and draws

heavily on his Gifts. The portal that forms is oval in shape and swirls with gray and blue smoke. It doesn't show a particular location yet because Shadow has not given it a destination. It is easier to maintain a portal if it's leaning on something, so Shadow moves the portal left until it reaches the back wall of the house.

"Thank you again. For everything," says Akuna.

"You and your family should come with us," Daniel says.

Akuna takes a small step backward like she expects Daniel to pick her up and throw her through the portal.

"This is our home," she whispers. The lantern near the door lights up her face and shines off the tears she's holding back. "We will not watch our city bow to hatred in silence. You must fight the way you know how, and we will do the same. Go with the Lady's blessing."

Seeing the strain on Shadow's face, Daniel echoes the woman's last farewell.

His mission is complete, and it's time to help Shadow. Daniel steps through the portal with Shadow close behind.

Their next stop is Aridel.

Chapter 6:
First Encounter

Katrina Polani
Village of New Haven

Our travels to Coolwater Creek are uneventful. We arrive early afternoon and stop to rest in one of the small taverns. Vic doesn't speak to us much. I think she's still upset about her father leaving her in our care once again. Shadow's contract to guard Daniel Saveron helps, but not by much. Tellen and Sara make half-hearted attempts to cheer Vic, but they quickly conclude that giving her space to deal with her grief is for the best.

Our meal consists of fresh bread and hot venison steaks with baked potatoes. It's the first good meal we've had since that last supper in Coldhaven several days ago, so we savor it. The table chatter around us seems ordinary. A man complains about zombies infesting the field he wants to plant peas in soon. A woman mentions that she hopes her husband returns from New Haven with the new blanket her mother had promised to have ready for her. The serving girl talks about her hope to visit Bastion one day.

I leave the task of filling the air around our table to Tellen and Sara. They take turns sharing short, amusing personal tales. My people don't trust strangers easily. I do not know Sara Andari well enough to open up just yet, but I enjoy hearing about her adventures as the village child minder and tutor. Tellen shares stories from his days training to become a huntsman. There are many parallels I could draw to my own training conducted by Master Talini, though my training was private and Tellen's was in a group setting.

Afterwards, we thank Vic. It's her treat since the money to purchase the meal came from her father. She shrugs off the thanks, but at least it earns a small smile.

The trek to the traveler's portal located a short ways north of the village passes quickly. Vic reaches it first but dutifully waits. She's under strict orders not to enter the portal first. We've no way of knowing what lies beyond. Generally, portal travel is safe, but these are not ordinary times. Bandits sometimes set up camp just outside a portal to ambush the travelers who step through. It rarely happens this close to a village, but we're not in the mood to take chances.

As planned, I step through first. Instinct causes me to take my snake form. Vic comes through next and her bracers light up.

The field around us hosts a pitched battle. Off to my right, several zombies kick at a fallen man. To my left, three men wave swords at a party of seven zombies huddled in front of a cowering figure clutching a scroll.

At least six more small battles take place near me, but I focus on the largest conflict centered around the figure with the scroll. Two zombies have already lost an arm each. Zipping between the men, I wrap my snake form around the nearest zombie's leg and yank it off by abruptly changing direction. I repeat this process a few times, toppling the lot of them in a matter of seconds. That's the extent of my ability to help. If we were in the woods I could help more because the trees would allow me to do the same maneuver by wrapping myself around the zombies' necks. Nevertheless, it's enough because Tellen and Vic arrive to finish them off. Tellen's daggers weave a deadly path through the fallen zombies before obediently returning to him. Blasts of pure energy from Vic's bracers dazzle every eye and reduce the remaining zombies to dust.

The men freeze.

With the zombies defeated, I study the men we aided. They are Arkonai but not ordinary huntsmen. I can tell that from the competent way they handle their long swords. Most huntsmen fight with daggers or bows. Swords aren't easy to haul around on long hunts. The men have pale skin that shows off the black marks they've painted on their faces. They keep their hair longer than most Arkonai, though it is confined at the back of their heads with simple thongs.

I return to human form.

The man nearest the huddled figure sheathes his sword and draws a small weapon from a leather holder on his belt. I gasp as the man points the weapon at the figure.

"No!" Vic's shout contains horror and fear.

A sharp crack like thunder explodes out of the weapon.

The kneeling figure cries out and collapses. I take to snake form and coil defensively. The nine other men arrange themselves in a loose semicircle standing between us and their leader.

Vic rushes forward but stops short of a wall of swords leveled at her. Once again, I initiate a change to human form and step to Vic's side. Tellen and Sara are already there holding her back.

"Step aside!" Vic sounds mad enough to walk right into a sword.

The men laugh but quickly sober. I don't detect any words but they part like soldiers issued a command. With five men moving left and four moving right, we soon have a clear view. The leader kicks the fallen figure onto its back.

The figure is a young woman barely older than me. The hood of her cloak has fallen aside, revealing her dark hair and empty eyes. She is beyond our help. Anger and sorrow strikes me at the same time. Tears blur my vision but I manage to stay on my feet.

This dead stranger was Saroth. My people will not react well when they hear of it. An incident like this could explode into open war. That is something the world cannot afford right now.

"Why would ya end such a precious life?" Sara asks softly.

"Wise up, girl," says a man standing to our left. "This type of evil has walked among our kind for too long."

His accent prompts me to take a closer look. These men—the followers—look like Arkonai and carry themselves like warriors, but they are Bereft. Only the leader is truly Arkonai. If the Resolute are training Bereft to do their bidding, the situation could be far worse than I'd imagined.

"Come to yer senses," urges a different man.

"Go home, children," says a third man.

"Turn over the Saroth girl and you can go in peace," offers the leader. He's a head taller than the men he commands. Calmly, he fiddles with the small weapon in his hands.

I've never seen anything like it before but the damage it can do is clear.

"Not a chance," Tellen snaps.

For a fleeting moment, I consider the proposition. If these men really want to fight us, there's a chance at least one of us won't walk away, likely Sara or me. Vic's bracers would defend her, and Tellen's by far the most competent fighter among us. I quickly banish the thought of surrender. I can't prevent a war while dead.

"Leave." Vic's voice holds enough command that a few of the men start to turn away before narrowing their eyes and planting their feet more firmly. She stares at the leader. When she speaks again, her tone and words shift to something beyond her. "Lay down your weapons and beg forgiveness from the One. He may spare your souls because you act in ignorance."

Once again, I do not hear an audible order, but the men charge Vic. Tellen grabs her shoulders and hauls her back. At the same time, her bracers light up and lengthen into sharp points that extend beyond her hands the distance of a short sword. She throws her arms wide, parrying two blows from separate enemies. Tellen uses the momentum of falling backward to toss Vic over his head toward me. Then, he leaps to his feet from a prone position and tosses a handful of lightning beams at the men's feet.

The move halts their progress only a moment. Tellen's twin daggers cross to catch a heavy sword strike. He pushes hard and knocks his opponent off balance. I turn into a dog and finish knocking the man over. A sword swings toward my head. Having no time to dodge, I turn into a beetle and dive underneath the flashing blade. Once that danger passes, I soar higher to get a sense of the battlefield.

Sara retreats to the side but two men close in on her. Vic flails about knocking numerous sword strikes aside. Nothing can touch her. Tellen drives a fist into one man's nose and slaps another with the flat side of his left dagger. He's trying very hard not to kill these men, and I admire him for it.

The leader stands back with his arms crossed. Seeing that his men have no lasting effect on us, he makes a subtle slicing motion. Instantly, the men withdraw. A few of them nurse nicks from Tellen's daggers, and at least one is limping. I've never heard of Arkonai having such precise control over the minds of men. Only the most daring—and crazy—of Minders would even consider such an intrusion into another's thoughts.

Descending, I take my human form. The leader shoots me a hate-filled glare before concentrating on Vic and Tellen.

"Our work here is done. What you do is your business, but I'd suggest you quit the company of that one immediately," the leader advises.

I bristle, not liking being referred to as "that one."

"Yer hatred will only lead ya astray," says Sara. "Release these men. What ye do is not right."

"My name is Corbin Vashtal of Urdik." The man speaks directly to Tellen and Vic. "Remember it and know that when I raise a larger force, I will cleanse the land of every Saroth I find."

In response to another hand motion, the men sheath their swords and form two lines. The leader sprints away and his men jog after him.

I look to my companions to see if we'll pursue them, but I see that, like me, they've no heart for such a chase. Sara's muttering prayers under her breath. Tellen grimly watches the retreating men. Vic rushes over to the young woman's body. On slightly unsteady feet, I cross to where Vic kneels. She places both hands over the large wound in the woman's chest. Gentle light pulses out of Vic's bracers. A small chunk of metal comes up out of the wound and lands in Vic's right hand. Her left hand presses over the wound, and the flesh knits itself together. A low moan comes from the woman.

"Impossible," I mutter.

"Nothing lies beyond the power of the One," Sara whispers, stepping up beside me. "Our Father—our Papa—can do all things. Ye have witnessed miracles before. I suspect if we stick with young Victoria we shall see much more."

I nod and watch Vic complete the healing. The young Saroth woman remains unconscious, but Tellen scoops her up and starts toward the distant village.

Chapter 7:
Sorrow Falls

Victoria Saveron
Village of New Haven

New Haven lies farther from its traveler's portal than most villages. If I'm recalling my portals lesson from Lady Gann correctly, that is because it's one of the first ever created. The Minder who fashioned it feared what would happen if he placed it too close to the village. He wasn't sure he could contain the amount of energy required to create a portal.

I don't consider myself a particularly observant person, and the recent fight has distracted me even more. Still, we're practically in the village before the sights and sounds truly hit me. Nearly every home trails smoke. Most dwellings are crumbling ruins. The place rumbles with waves of collective grief punctuated by high-pitched wails. It makes me think perhaps we're about to meet a horde of the undead.

The expressions worn by my companions tell me they're bracing for the worst. Tellen leads us around the corner of the Gathering Hall where we find nearly every citizen of New Haven. Some mill about with emptiness in their eyes. Others weep on the ground. A few children quietly play in the moist dirt near the well. Everybody stops moving when they see us.

A neat line of ten bodies stretches across our path. The few closest to me bear wounds similar to the one I just healed. I want to act, but these souls are beyond my help.

"What happened? Where are the village elders?" I don't even realize I'm speaking until a woman answers me.

"There," says an old woman, pointing to the bodies. Her eyes are red-rimmed and bloodshot with grief. "Most of the old elders are there. New Haven is no more. Ye have entered Sorrow Falls."

A child cries out in fright and buries his head in his mother's skirt. She stoops to see what has frightened him. After listening a second, her head whips up and she glares at Tellen before saying something I can't hear to the man standing next to her. The crowd's mood shifts, buzzing with agitation.

"They're with them!" mutters a young man.

"They're here to kill us!" wails a woman.

Tellen quickly places the woman he's been carrying on the ground behind him and steps forward. Four village men rush to meet him, ready to fight. The rest of the people shrink away from us.

"I take it we're not welcome here," Tellen murmurs to us.

Katrina makes a noise that agrees with him while also conveying her annoyance at his attempt at levity. She steps up beside him. The sight of her makes the four village men halt abruptly.

"Papa, she's like Nina," says a child.

Katrina's dark hair and olive skin help identify her as a Saroth, but that alone would not be conclusive proof. I'm not sure what caused the child to make that observation, except perhaps the way my friend carefully watches everything around her.

"Is Nina dead? Did they kill her?"

I can't identify which woman spoke this time. There are too many people in the way.

"Who are you and why are you here?" inquires one of the men. His tone is challenging yet curious.

"We're just passing through," says Sara. She kneels by the Saroth woman called Nina. "We wanted to pick up supplies before heading to the Alamon Temple."

"There's nothing to be had here," comments the first woman who spoke. She introduces herself as Willow Ezard, wife of the recently deceased Elder Myron Ezard. "We've just finished voting on our new name. It is the last formal act before leaving."

"A hundred undead are coming for us!" calls a boy. He sounds excited by the prospect.

"Where will you go?" I wonder.

"South toward Temperance," says Willow.

The man who first demanded we identify ourselves repeats his wishes. Tellen handles our introductions, but I don't pay much attention to them. Still, I'm aware enough to hear that the man's name is Ryle

Ezard, son of Myron and Willow. Unlike his mother, Ryle speaks without much of the lilting accent I've come to expect from Bereft villagers. I get the feeling Ryle's spent much time away from this tiny village.

A sense of responsibility settles upon me like a heavy cloak.

"We're going with you." My statement shocks the villagers and my companions.

"Vic, we need to travel fast," Katrina protests.

"They need our protection," I explain. Certainty like I've never felt before fills me. "They'll die if we leave them now." I silently beg Tellen and Sara for support.

"Why should we let you travel with us?" Ryle demands.

"Peace, Ryle. There is something special about her." Willow's gray eyes study me.

"Mother, we can't trust them," Ryle hisses. "They travel with an Arkonai." His suspicious glare lands on Tellen.

"I am not your enemy," Tellen assures Ryle. "The ones you speak of are a small cult among my people. They call themselves Resolute, but they do not represent all Arkonai."

Ryle scoffs.

"There's nothing small about the group that passed through here yesterday," he says bitterly. He struggles a moment, trying to hold more words in, but the effort fails. "Where were the rest of your people when those beasts swept through here on their witch hunt yesterday? Where were you when they filled the Gathering Hall this morning and murdered the elders?"

"Blaming us is not going to solve your problems," Katrina notes. "Vic wants to help you, but we cannot force you to accept our aid."

"How can she help us?" Ryle challenges. His anger seeps away, leaving him weary. "She's just a child."

"She's also blessed by the One," says Sara.

I sense a question in Sara's steady gaze and nod, giving her permission to continue. Leaving Nina's side, Sara comes over and picks up my hand. I'd been hiding the right one in a small rag to keep people from noticing its unnatural gray color. My bracers are in their thin, bracelet form, but when Sara slides her hands over them, they lengthen and cover my forearms. Sunlight glints off the shiny silver surface making them golden.

A new wave of shock rolls through the crowd. Several whispers have the phrase "Chosen Redeemer" in them. The title doesn't make me uncomfortable like it once did, but I suddenly wish to be alone. Fear of the crowd makes my breaths come quicker. My vision blurs and I expect to pass out.

"Say something, Victoria," Sara whispers. She's behind me now. Gripping my upper arms hard, she speaks directly into my left ear. "You have their attention. Give their hearts the courage they need. Remind them of Papa's love. My prayers are with thee."

How can I give anybody courage when I have none?

A brave toddler dashes out from the crowd, which now forms a circle around us. My Arkonai and Saroth friends tense like they expect the child to attack us. The boy gazes up at me in wonder and stretches out his small arms. Dropping low, I let him grasp the metal bracers. He giggles, babbles something, and hugs me. I stand to relieve my burning knees and pick up the child as I rise. I form a bench with my left arm and hold him in place with my right, turning him to face the crowd.

"You will always have what you need." The Lady tucks the words into my mind.

Peace sweeps over me like a warm breeze, first falling upon my face, then down my arms, and finally flowing to the rest of me. The child in my arms must feel it too for he sighs with contentment.

"Dark times are coming," I begin, "but even at your lowest point you will always find a reason to hope, a reason to fight." I tighten my embrace around the toddler. He coos in response. Comforted, I raise my eyes to the crowd again. "The Darkland creatures are our real enemies. The rest of the strife that exists is foolishness. It has roots in a few selfish people grasping for power. Don't let them divide you. If your neighbor is Saroth, welcome her. If a huntsman seeks shelter, give it to him. Let the pain of loss unite you. Let no man—or woman—tell you who to hate or what to fear. Look to the Lady and the One for guidance and peace."

Many in the crowd agree with me.

"Will ye stay with us?" asks Willow Ezard.

"I will stay for now," I answer cautiously, "but my path may diverge from yours. I will not know until the time comes."

The announcement satisfies the crowd enough for them to disperse. Ryle doesn't look happy that we're staying, but he keeps the opinion to himself. Most of the men pick up swords and axes to gather wood to burn the bodies. The ground's too hard to dig enough holes for the dead. Many of the women work from the few undamaged homes to bake enough bread and cook enough meat to feed everybody.

Tellen moves Nina into the Gathering Hall where Willow Ezard has set up a quiet area to dress wounds. Willow directs him to place the young woman by her father, the only elder to survive the confrontation yesterday and the purge this morning. A man stands guard outside the door, keeping most of the people out. Sara helps the women while Katrina and I stand by in the hopes of speaking with Elder Roman Piccard, a rare Saroth born Bereft. That explains the natural sympathy for Saroth that exists within the people of Sorrow Falls.

While we wait, Willow describes what led to the massacre. A band of about twenty-five Resolute rode in on horses, followed by dozens of Bereft men armed with swords. The riders each had one of the new weapons that fire pieces of metal from short, stick-like barrels. Some of the village men tried to resist but were quickly overwhelmed. The leader of the Resolute, Huntmaster Galeric, demanded that Nina and her father be surrendered.

Alerted to the trouble, Nina had been sent away mere hours before. The attackers held the elders hostage for hours while the Resolute questioned Roman on the whereabouts of his daughter. Roman couldn't fight his tormentors, but he repeatedly refused to give in. Finally, Galeric had his men burn several houses in an effort to draw Nina out. When that failed, he spread the word that the elders would die at dawn if Nina couldn't be found.

To save themselves, the elders told Galeric where to find Nina. That's when the man ordered their deaths. The Bereft soldiers forced the villagers to watch the executions. Roman was to be last, but something caused Galeric to change his plans. He ordered one of his men to stay behind and continue the search for Nina. That was the small party we met recently.

Katrina looks unsettled, but before I can speak with her Tellen pulls her aside. With her story finished, Willow leaves to organize the people and answer their questions. She has inherited the right to rule from her dead husband. I am left alone with Nina and her father. Since they're both unconscious, it's not much of a conversation. I try to pray for them, but my heart hurts too much to leave room for words.

With half the houses uninhabitable and a force of undead approaching, the people will need to flee south. I know I have a mission to fulfill, but I need to help them. When Shadow returns with my father they can take us directly to the Alamon Temple. Until then, we would be stuck traveling on foot anyway.

Chapter 8:
Resolute Recruit

The Lady
Portal to the Home of Lady Christa, City of Aridel
Emerging from the portal, Daniel Saveron and Shadow are immediately confronted by two huntsmen.

"Halt," commands the younger of the two. His hand hovers near a sword but he does not draw it. "State your business."

"I've come to visit my mother," Shadow explains.

"And who is your mother?" inquires the older portal guardian.

"Lady Christa," Shadow answers.

"Shadow? Is it really you?" calls the younger man. He relaxes slightly. "Who stands with you?"

"I have come with Huntsman Seeker Daniel Saveron," says Shadow. "We're here for a brief visit with my mother, nothing more."

The guards stiffen at Daniel's name, but they make no move to stop the pair.

"You'd best hurry then," comments the older guard. "The Supreme Huntmaster arrived a few minutes before you did. I don't know what business he has with Lady Christa, but he seemed in a hurry."

The paths winding through Aridel are narrower but better lit than those in Urdik. Intent on their mission, Daniel and Shadow cannot appreciate the beauty. If viewed from afar, the city glows like a candle-covered mountain. Soft lanterns light up the paths at regular intervals, allowing them to sprint up the winding ways. Shadow leads since he knows exactly where to go. It has been many ages since Daniel set foot in Aridel, but once upon a time, he had called it home.

Sweet and painful memories strike Daniel upon seeing the lovely marble statues lining the courtyard of Soaring Oaks. Christa retreated to her childhood home when her husband became the Supreme Huntmaster. Guilt hits Daniel hard.

I should have been there for her.

At the time he'd been mired in his own troubles brought on by his forbidden marriage to Marina Castaloni. Still, he'd once been Christa's best friend. He should have helped regardless of the consequences.

Heedless of Daniel's reservations, Shadow blazes to the front door and sails through, barely pausing to open the door. A portly servant clutches her chest and gasps.

"Master Shadow! What brings ye here at this hour?" she asks. "Oh, ya gave me a fright, ya did!"

"Where is my mother?" Shadow's tone has an imperious snap to it. He adjusts his tone to add, "Please, Annie, I need to see her."

Annie wrings her hands.

"Master Jordan said they were not to be disturbed for any reason."

Throwing back the hood of his cloak, Daniel steps forward and grips the old woman's hands.

"Annie, the Supreme Huntmaster's about to go on a holy war. She could be in danger."

"Master Daniel! Oh, I've not seen ye for years!" The delight disappears quickly. "Is it true?"

"He would not be here for any other reason," says Shadow gravely.

"Come." Annie starts to lead the way but Shadow stops her.

"Gather the servants," he instructs. "Go to the chapel and pray for my mother. We will find her." He waits for Annie to rush off before turning to Daniel. "Can you sense her? There are two places we're likely to find her but they're in opposite directions."

"I can find her," Daniel assures Shadow.

Closing his eyes, Daniel quiets his spirit and silently reaches out to sense his friend. A sharp, hot sensation slices through his heart, telling him Christa's in distress. Without explaining, he follows the feeling through many rooms out into the back courtyard.

When they arrive, they find Lady Christa kneeling next to a large fountain with a statue representing Kailon—which means Eternal King—reaching out to bring life to Aeris.

She is not alone.

Three huntsmen nervously stand nearby. They draw weapons when Shadow and Daniel stop inside the garden.

"Get out," Shadow orders. He knows their purpose. These are the witnesses his father brought to shore up his resolve.

According to tradition, a true warrior embarking on Nerulic Victis would cut ties to his past by sacrificing something or someone he treasures. The tradition carried on in a less bloody manner for the office of the Supreme Huntmaster. Symbolically, that is what happened when Jordan Lekros left his wife when she was pregnant with Shadow and his twin sister, Dina. Modern Arkonai defend the tradition by saying that it prevents loved ones from being used to manipulate the Supreme Huntmaster. But with Jordan's newfound devotion to the Resolute, I fear he may kill Christa. I believe that was his purpose here, but something changed.

Cautiously, Shadow crosses to his mother and leans over to check if she's safe. Daniel resists the urge to go to them and watches the three would-be witnesses, Huntsman Vivek, Huntmaster Crane, and Huntmaster Leon. Prior to this moment, he's known they had traditionalist tendencies, but he never would have guessed they would cast their lot with the Resolute.

"There will be no sacrifice today," he tells them. "You should leave this place."

"Where did the Supreme Huntmaster go?" asks Huntsman Vivek, sounding dazed.

Daniel would like that question answered too, but Christa looks in no condition to explain.

"He left," answers Huntmaster Crane, speaking more to himself than the others. "He left with the girl." He mutters a curse. "She might as well be Saroth with that black magic she pulled."

I'm tempted to urge Daniel to look back in time, but he cannot afford such a distraction right now. It's unlikely these three will attack him, but the times are strange enough for the unexpected to happen.

Shadow has exchanged quiet words with his mother. He now stands and faces the three men. His stiff posture displays the anger hidden beneath his mask.

"None who follow the Resolute are welcome here," he declares.

"The Supreme Huntmaster can go where he pleases," retorts Huntmaster Crane. "Besides, he still has a legal claim to the property."

"Do you see him here?" Shadow barks. "Because I don't. He's

gone, and he's not likely to return."

"The last word on the matter belongs to the lady of the house," says Daniel, trying to get the three to leave before young Shadow's patience disappears. "Why don't we hear her out?"

Shadow helps his mother up from her kneeling position and lowers her to a seat on the fountain's edge. Christa has changed much in the years since Daniel last saw her, but he still recognizes the way her long blond hair curls near the ends. Her green eyes peer at him for a long second before moving on to the three intruders. Wiping away tears, Christa draws herself up regally.

"Gentlemen, my son speaks truth. You will not find your Supreme Huntmaster here. Return to Bastion and await his word. That is the best you can hope for. Now, if you'll excuse me, I'd like a word with my son and Seeker Daniel."

Tension slowly builds. Finally, Huntmaster Leon bows to Lady Christa and backs away. The others retreat similarly until they reach the door and exit.

Daniel studies his friend and crosses the tiny garden to stand before her. They exchange awkward greetings before Daniel overcomes his shyness and pulls her into a hug. They break apart when Shadow clears his throat and asks his mother to explain the incident with his father and sister.

"I didn't even know you had a daughter," says Daniel.

"Neither did Jordan," Christa points out. She turns away to look into the gentle water flowing from the fountain. Her shoulders dip and her head bows. She lets several heartbeats pass. "Her name is Dina, and she is Shadow's twin, my firstborn by minutes."

"Why did you hide her from Jordan?" Daniel inquires. He's careful to keep condemnation out of the question.

"I don't know," Christa answers. More time passes. She organizes her thoughts and lets the water run between her fingers. "I think the reason has changed over the years." Turning, Christa sits on the fountain's edge again. She motions for Daniel and Shadow to be seated, but they remain standing. "At first, I was angry with him for abandoning me. Then, I was angry with him for ignoring Devin." A bitter smile crosses her lips. "Then, I was angry with him for taking Devin away from me."

"I see that is not the reason now," Daniel prompts.

Christa nods.

"As she grew I saw inklings of what her Gifts would be. I hired both Saroth and Arkonai tutors to train her in secret, and she excelled in every way, even beyond her brother because her training was more focused." Christa holds a hand out to Shadow and he takes it. Pain and sorrow hang on each of her words. "Now, I fear what she's become."

"And what is that?" Daniel wonders, keeping his voice at whisper level.

"She's a Portal Master," says Christa, "or will be very soon." She retrieves her hand from Shadow's grasp.

"We need to find her," Shadow murmurs. "She could help us."

"She won't," Christa counters.

"Why do you say that?" Daniel asks.

"Because I think she may be Resolute." Tears shine in Christa's eyes. "Tonight, she was waiting for Jordan to come. She was excited. Only at the last moment did she whisk him away before he could carry out his mission." At these words, Christa studies the rough rope burns marking both wrists. The discarded pieces of rope litter the nearby ground.

"We will find her anyway," Daniel promises. "Perhaps you misread her intentions."

"If her powers have grown that much, she might be difficult to track down," Shadow cautions. "I can create portals to connect to the existing traveler's portals, and in special cases, I might be able to connect to a place without a portal. If I'm lucky, I can take one or two other people with me." He lets Daniel absorb the words before finishing the explanation. "If Dina is a Portal Master, she can create and destroy them at will. She could move whole armies."

"You have to save her from herself," says Christa. She gazes up at Shadow. "Take off your mask, Devin. I need to see your face."

He does so, and Daniel finally sees the real Shadow. The sandy brown hair and brown eyes are much like the boy Jordan was once upon a time. Daniel half-expects his friend's voice to mock him for staring.

Christa pulls Shadow down until he kneels before her and cups his face with her hands.

"Stay here and train with Master Pedallo."

"I can't," Shadow whispers. "I have a Guardian contract with Seeker Daniel and his daughter. Victoria is the Lady's Chosen Redeemer. I have sworn to protect her."

Two tears slip out, but Christa bows her head, accepting Shadow's words.

"If Dina's with the Resolute, we will meet her eventually," Daniel notes. "I can speak for no other, but I will do what I can for her." He places a hand on Christa's shoulder.

She drops her hands from around Shadow's face and folds them in her lap.

"That is all I can ask, but will you stay with me a while? You should at least stop and refresh yourselves. I see that the road has been long and hard, and I suspect it may be longer still."

Seeing the wisdom in this, Daniel and Shadow agree to rest for the night. They will need to reunite with Victoria soon, but they will be better able to help her if they have their strength. If her party meets no resistance and travels at top speed, they should reach the Alamon Temple in a couple of weeks, sooner if they manage to find horses. Shadow's Gift will allow Daniel to travel there in a matter of minutes. If he knew exactly where to find Victoria, he might try to meet her along the way, but there aren't many villages between Midpoint and the temple. With Shadow's Gift limited largely to established portals, they are better off waiting in safety until it's time to meet her.

Chapter 9:
Relentless Pursuit

Katrina Polani
Plains of Forgiveness, Path to the Alamon Temple
Our journey nears the three week anniversary. If we'd traveled alone we might have reached the Alamon Temple by now, but Vic is right. These people would not survive long without us. Sara has taken to entertaining and teaching the children. Vic's picked up the ability to sense parties of undead so we can steer the refugee column around them or at least deal with them before anybody gets hurt. In addition, Tellen's training the men to fight, and I'm helping the hunting parties track down enough food for everybody.

The new weapon Corbin Vashtal wielded against us near the Sorrow Falls Portal fascinates Tellen. He contacted his father when we reached Midpoint and obtained two of the things along with the metal slugs called bullets that come out of them. He spends each evening training the men to fight with swords and bows before learning to use the guns along with Sara, Vic, and me. He's by far the most proficient with the weapon, but I think Sara's skill is improving nicely too. Vic and I are useless with guns. The thunderous crack that comes from the weapon unnerves Vic, and I always hesitate when aiming because I keep picturing the damage Corbin's gun did to Nina Piccard.

She's awake now, but she spends nearly every moment at her father's side tending to his wounds. At least one of the blades that struck him must have been poisoned for the healing to progress this slowly. I've only spoken with Nina a few times. Despite her Conjurer abilities, she possesses the mindset of an ordinary Bereft. Her control over her creations is mediocre at best because she has no formal training. The zombies she set against Corbin and his men were born out of fear. That shows me she has tremendous power, but it also proves that there's danger in letting Gifts blossom without direction and training. Perhaps we will find a suitable tutor for her at the temple, but I'm not even certain she will tolerate a tutor.

Each day is long and tiring, but good. There's a sense of accomplishment and fulfillment in teaching, learning, and living beside these Bereft people. Most days I can forget that evil men want to destroy my people, or that the Outcast still has followers unlocking Darkland portals every chance they can. The days we trip over a party of zombies, that's a little harder, but this is the most peace we've experienced since fleeing Vic's home in the Karnok Mountains.

I patrol the camp several times each night, anticipating dawn. Tellen's made a game of finding me each morning. Some days I let him spot me and others I fly down in beetle form and transform very close to him. Occasionally, I have the pleasure of shaking that perpetual Arkonai calm. I enjoy both the mornings we spend in idle chatter and the ones we watch the sunrise in silence.

This morning is different. Tellen's movements are stiff with agitation.

"Katrina," he calls softly, trying not to awaken everybody.

His urgency demands that I focus, so I fly over to him and initiate the change.

"I am here," I answer, landing on my feet. "What can I do for you?"

"Fly up and look northwest toward the Silver Springs Forest," Tellen instructs. "Tell me what you see."

His tone indicates that he already knows what I'll see.

Curious, I comply. Once again taking on beetle form, I shoot straight up into the sky. When I'm several hundred feet off the ground, I fly a few slow loops. When my eyes fall upon the direction Tellen spoke of, I see faint smoke trails beyond the far side of the forest. Diving down to Tellen, I change back and relay my findings.

"We need to leave," Tellen says, speaking swiftly.

"I'll start getting people up," I offer.

He catches my arm.

"You and me," Tellen clarifies.

"We can't leave Vic," I protest.

"We have to." Tellen's never looked more serious. "I spotted those pursuers two days ago. That's why I insisted we go without fires. I thought we might be able to slip away and lengthen the lead, but that hasn't happened. If I'm right, that's the party of Resolute that almost killed Nina and her father. If they're caught again, they'll die. You and I are the only ones who can draw the Resolute away and possibly escape."

"Vic won't like it." I don't like it, but I know he's right.

"We're not going to tell her," says Tellen. "We're going to tell Sara and let her tell Vic later. Can you do that? You stand a much better chance of sneaking into the women's area than I do."

In that much, he speaks truth.

"I'll grab supplies and let Ryle know. He can tell his mother. Meet me back here in five minutes." Tellen races off before I can answer.

I use beetle form to fly over to the small tent Sara and Vic share with several children. Entering the tent, I change back to human form. I'd rather not be smacked should one of the children mistake me for an ordinary bug. Luckily, Sara's a light sleeper and a gentle tap on her shoulder returns her to consciousness. I cover her mouth to prevent her from crying out.

"We're leaving," I say. "Tellen spotted trouble behind the column. We're going to draw it away from the people. If everything goes well, we will meet you at the temple. Tell Vic when you can." Shifting my hand away from her mouth, I pause to see if she's awake enough to understand. "And … pray for us."

"Lady go with thee." Sara grips my arm and squeezes to assure me my message is received.

A quick flight brings me back to where I'd met Tellen earlier. He's already there with Ryle.

"Let me come with you," Ryle pleads. "I can fight. Let us battle these devils together."

Tellen shakes his head.

"Keep practicing. You'll need those fighting skills soon enough." He claps Ryle on the left shoulder. "Katrina and I can handle this, but just in case, get the people moving soon. Go into the Dancing Woods Forest if you have to. I know the huntsman there. His name is Ezra. He will help you."

Tellen tosses me a loaf of bread and a filled waterbag and begins jogging away from the camp.

"What am I supposed to do with this?" I ask, looking down at the loaf of bread. I sling the waterbag over my shoulder.

"That's your morning meal." Tellen jogs backwards for a few

steps. "Sorry you'll have to eat on the run."

Shrugging, I turn to dog form, consume the bread in a few bites, and sprint to catch up. There aren't many advantages to being a Shapeshifter, but running faster than normal humans—even Arkonai—is definitely one of them. Were it not for the notion that we're headed for grave danger, I would enjoy the run.

I've not raced full-speed in dog form for ages. Long ago, I challenged my friend, Dorian Camporello, to a race from his house to mine, a distance of twenty kilometers. His main animal form is that of a panther. He wanted to prove the superiority of cat forms over dog forms. For a long time, he maintained a solid lead, but eventually, the distance worked in my favor. I've not thought about Dorian for a long time.

When we've put a couple of hours of distance between us and the refugee column, Tellen stops and rests by walking in slow circles with his hands clasped above his head. We've reached the edge of the Silver Springs Forest. I change out of dog form to drink water and settle into a cross-legged position to watch him think.

I feel an important conversation coming and begin preparing arguments to things he might bring up. The instant before he speaks, I glean that he wishes to send me away.

"Go back, Katrina. Let me handle this." There's anguish in his blue eyes, and he's paler than usual.

"What do you intend to do?" I ask carefully, squashing the urge to say something flippant.

"I'll stall them with lightning traps." Tellen waves to indicate the thick trees that lie ahead of us.

Spotting a line of low bushes heavily laden with small, round berries gives me an idea. I don't like the idea of destroying the forest, but I'm desperate to keep this horde away from Vic.

"I can set traps too," I assure Tellen. I create a small flame with my right fingertips, reminding him of the Saroth Gift for controlling fire.

"Using what?" Tellen asks. "I don't think a campfire's up to the task here."

I wave to the bushes.

"Don't you recognize them?" A wicked grin comes to me easily.

Whirling, Tellen spots the baydonberry bushes.

"You can't be serious," he mutters. "You'll burn down the whole forest."

"I don't believe there are that many baydonberry bushes, but it should be enough to slow them down," I say.

My Arkonai accomplice doesn't look pleased with our plan but he races headlong into the woods. We don't have much time. We need to reach the far side of the Silver Springs Forest before our enemies enter. The traps will take time to put into place. Silently begging the One for forgiveness for what we're about to do, I take on my snake form and forge a quick path through the trees.

Chapter 10:
Desperate Flight

Victoria Saveron
Sorrow Falls Temporary Camp, Plains of Forgiveness

Sara Andari wakes me up like she does every morning, but today is different. Her grip upon my left shoulder is fiercer than normal. One glance at her expression convinces me I'm not going to like whatever she has to say. The look contains grief, compassion, and deep conviction. Forcing myself to a sit up, I brace for her news, yet it still hits me hard.

"I was asked to bear a message, and I wish it were not so," she begins. "Trouble comes behind us. Katrina and Tellen have gone to meet it in our stead."

"Where are they?" I ask, throwing off my blanket.

Sara makes a calming gesture.

"They are well on their way."

The quietness in the tent suddenly strikes me. We're completely alone. With few tents and hundreds of people such a thing would never simply happen.

"You waited to awaken me." My words are part accusation and part statement.

"Ye would have stopped them," Sara explains. "And they would have listened, and the trouble they face would strike us all."

Knowing she's right does little to tame the helpless anger coursing through me. I clench my hands and jaw to keep in words I'll regret. The frustration creates angry tears. Sara's wise enough to give me a moment to process my feelings. Her closed eyes tell me she's praying. Fear for Tellen and Katrina tightens across my chest, making breathing

49

difficult. I try to pray, but the worry leaves my mind blank.

If I don't move soon, I may lose the will to move again. Struggling to my feet, I stumble toward the tent entrance.

"Victoria, wait!" Sara calls. "There's more!"

Ignoring her, I step out of the tent and nearly slam into Ryle Ezard and his mother, Willow. What looks like the rest of the village stands just beyond them. Besides this tent, everything else has been bundled up or loaded onto one of the four horse-drawn wagons. Men, women, and children stare at me from a short distance behind Ryle and Willow. I can't see behind the tent, but I'm fairly certain there are people back there too.

As I rock back on my heels, Sara steadies my shoulders.

"I meant to warn ye," she whispers. "They seek answers from ya."

There's nowhere I can escape such a crowd. It's my worst nightmare coming true.

"What should we do?" asks Ryle.

I've never seen the big man this subdued. The shift in attitude is frightening. I don't understand why he's asking me what to do.

"About what?" I wonder. I brush my hands over my face to wipe away the tears. The sun's rising behind the distant Dancing Woods Forest.

Ryle waves and two men step forward. Mikkel Black and Caleb Anderson have taken up much of the scouting duties. Both men are sweating despite the chilly morning air.

Mikkel reports first. His right hand forms a fist and crosses over his chest in a salute.

"There's a large force approaching from the northwest. The Arkonai and the Saroth will likely reach the Silver Springs Forest at the same time, but I'm not sure if they can slow down that many. My men estimate the force numbers between two and three hundred."

I blink, trying to understand why he's reporting to me. Tellen should be here to receive such a report. He'd know what to do. Guessing that Mikkel needs acknowledgement, I nod to let him know I've heard his words.

Mikkel drops his hand and takes a half-step back. Caleb does the opposite, stepping up and taking on the same pose Mikkel did.

"There are Darkland creatures coming out of the Dancing Woods Forest. Most are normal zombies, but there are kitsarue and even a few Denkari with them." Report finished, Caleb retreats until he's even with Mikkel.

"How many?" I direct the question to Caleb. My mind fixes on passages and sketches from my father's reference book: *Darkland Dangers: a Non-exhaustive Survey of the Fascinating and Deadly Creatures Living Beyond the Veil.* The author is a bit overly fond of words and absolutely obsessed with everything that has to do with the Darklands, but the book does a decent job of cataloging the things that occasionally crawl, claw, and spring from the Darklands.

Kitsarue are six-legged creatures that can run extremely fast for short distances. They can also walk upright like humans. Their middle pair of legs can morph into rigid, sword-like extensions. Their upper legs are more like hands, capable of wielding conventional weapons. Unlike zombies, they're intelligent creatures. They were created by the Outcast when he decided to rebel against Kailon. I think he based them on wolves from their elongated facial structures, but their body fur can excrete a liquid that hardens into a shell, creating armor that lasts a few hours at a time. The sketches always portray them with fierce snarls, but I wonder what lies behind their glowing red eyes. Do they feel pain like we do?

Denkari are spirit warriors. I believe they defected from Kailon's army, lured away by promises of power if they served the Outcast. The pictures depict them as tall, pale humans armed with spirit swords, but the book mentioned that they can also fling spirit shards or use weapons fashioned by men. Katrina, Tellen, and Shadow said the three Denkari they ran into in Coldhaven were pale, gaunt men with dead eyes. Denkari can drain one's will to fight with their minds or a toxin from their claws. Even one of those would be dangerous.

"At least a hundred," Caleb answers, pulling me from my reflections on kitsarue and Denkari.

Either force is large enough to destroy this column of refugees.

Every eye falls upon me.

As panic surges, I'm suddenly aware of Sara's hands gripping my shoulders. Heat radiates from the twin points of contact on my back. A spirit of peace settles over me. I'm still not sure how I ended up in this position, but if the One and the Lady will it, we shall save these people.

I consider the dangers. An army of men may only kill some of the people if we surrender when overtaken. The Darkland nightmares will probably murder everybody. Those aren't great options. Moving toward one army brings us away from the other. If we time it right, we may even be able to race ahead and have both enemies converge behind us. If they meet, they might take each other out. I know I'm stretching, but it's the best plan I can think of. I feel better equipped to face a supernatural army than one made up of men.

"Leave the wagons," I say, reaching a decision. I wish my voice didn't sound so young. "Spread out the supplies. Give each person a burden light enough to carry if they have to run. Unhitch the horses and get the best riders mounted. Divide the mobile force into three sections. These will travel to the left, right, and behind the main body of people. Everybody capable of holding a sword or a bow should arm themselves and line up at the front of the column. This is where Sara and I will be."

"What do you want the riders to do?" Mikkel asks.

"Have them keep a rotating circuit," I answer.

"What about the tents?" asks Willow.

The tents that have housed us for the past few weeks are large and heavy. They're waterproof and very protective but there's no way to carry them without the wagons.

"Cut them up," I say, surprising everybody. "We're a few days out from the Alamon Temple. We won't need them once we reach the temple. If you cut the tents into pieces small enough for each person to carry their own, they will at least have something to wrap themselves in at night." I doubt we'll be getting much rest for the next few days, but I keep that observation to myself.

Several men draw daggers and rush to the wagons to unpack and break down the tents. Other people move to get the horses prepared to hold riders, but the vast majority still stand before me waiting for orders.

"How should we arrange the people?" Ryle inquires.

I consider the question for a few beats before answering.

"Keep the children in the center and keep family groups together, but assign everybody a partner to watch over and protect. Give everybody a task, from the oldest to the youngest. Put the sick and infirm on horses in the center with the children. Tether them to the horses if you have to, or mount two people if the horse will bear them."

Ryle delegates specific tasks to the men and his mother organizes the women. Several sewing needles come out, and I'm assuming they're for creating makeshift capes for those too young to carry their share of the tents. Those details don't concern me. Turning to Sara, I study the Coldhaven woman. She's stuck with me this long, but I realize I've just volunteered her for one of the most dangerous positions in the column.

"I'll gladly stand with thee," Sara assures me. "Now come, we ought to get food into ya before the camp breaks down completely."

I hardly taste the two large slices of bread somebody hands me. Sara's already filled my waterbag, but I'm reluctant to drink too much from it since I'm not sure when we'll find a decent spring to fill them again. My thoughts churn, and I feel the weight of responsibility I've just accepted. Knowing Sara is constantly in a state of prayer helps, but my worry must show up on my face since a small child just burst into tears. I'll have to work on that. I can't help people if my expressions go about scaring them. Peace still exists in me. I'm just not certain how to project that.

The people of Sorrow Falls follow my instructions incredibly swiftly. Soon, we're on the move with me at the head of this ragged band. I aim for the Dancing Woods Forest.

Why do I feel like I'm marching everybody to their doom?

Chapter 11:
Jackson's Proposal

The Lady
Galeric's Camp near the Silver Springs

Jackson Castaloni has not been idle. He's been traveling the continent extensively. I have not been able to follow him to most meetings, but he keeps a convenient map on the wall of his chambers in Fort Medron. Although two visits were to Saroth cities, Dominance and Jorash, most were to Bereft villages and remote locations like the Desolate Mountains. I cannot fathom his motives yet. He keeps his mind unusually well-guarded. I can only assume he's following his master's mandate to cause chaos.

This trip is different. For one thing, he's brought Alec with him. While grateful for the opportunity to witness what comes, I'm not pleased that he's brought the boy into harm's way again. It's clear this is a military camp. The flags declare it belongs to the Resolute. I spread my presence thin to get a feel for the place. The mood is frenetic like these men are drunk on the need to fight. Sometimes this spills over into arguments and fistfights, but mostly, they trade boasts of one sort or another.

The Arkonai keep to themselves in a section to the right side of the camp, closest to the Purity Plains. Several huntsmen patrol the perimeter and walk through the Bereft section to maintain order where necessary.

I'm disheartened to see that there are women and children wandering throughout the camp serving the men an evening meal. The chains around their wrists and ankles declare them slaves. I spend a short time ministering to their low spirits before returning my attention to Alec and Jackson.

Soon, I understand why Jackson brought Alec. The boy darts forward until challenged by one of the Arkonai guards. Words are exchanged and a message is sent back to the central tent. In another moment, Alec is bound in chains and kneeling on the camp's edge with a solid wall of Arkonai and Bereft standing behind him.

The wall parts and a tall, powerfully built blond man strides through the gap. He places a massive hand on Alec's head and strokes the boy's dark hair. I keep Alec calm, but even without my help he would face the danger bravely since the One has given him a courageous spirit.

"The Lady must smile upon me tonight to have delivered such lovely gifts," says the tall man. A peek into his surface thoughts reveals him to be Huntmaster Galeric. A breeze off the Silver Springs lifts his free-flowing hair, creating a stream behind him.

"I seek a private audience with you." Jackson's tone conveys impatience. "We have much to discuss."

Galeric throws back his head and laughs. His men follow suit. He stops laughing abruptly, draws one of the guns strapped to his waist, and places the barrel at the base of Alec's neck.

"If this is a trap, it's a terrible one," he comments.

"It's no trap," Jackson assures the man. "That's why the boy is here. Your men can keep him until we conclude our business. Our talk will be completely within their sight, though out of the range of their ears."

The blond man tilts his head to the side and considers the proposal.

"How do I know the boy means something to you?" Galeric asks.

"You don't, but we have the same master," Jackson explains. "He's told me your purpose and bid me to help you, so here I am. If you send me away, you can explain why my aid was not received."

"What aid could you possibly give me, Saroth?" Galeric's question causes his men to voice their agreement, but he stills them by raising a hand. "Your kind is the cause of the troubles with the Darkland creatures. That is why we're destroying them in every village we pass through on the way to meet the undead."

"Come speak with me, and you will have your answers," says Jackson. "At this point, I care not. I will take my apprentice and leave you to wage war as you see fit."

"And the alternative?" Galeric presses.

"You step forward ten paces and allow me to use a privacy spell. Then, I will tell you a better use of the forces you've gathered."

The notion of a privacy spell frustrates me. I don't want to leave Alec, but if I don't, their discussion will be out of my reach. Deciding to risk it, I move my presence from Alec's mind into Galeric's thoughts. He's weighing Jackson's proposal seriously but leaning toward ordering his men to kill Jackson.

I am sorely tempted to urge him to take that path, but I know it would fail and many would die. These are bloodthirsty men and a violent end will likely be their fate someday, but such a move would place me on a path to serve the Outcast. I cannot and will not betray my master that way.

Galeric's mind brims with plans and parts of plans. He knows how to inspire men to do his bidding. That's how he has drawn such a large crowd of armed followers.

Subtly, I shift his mood to one of amusement. He slowly slides the gun back into its holster and yanks Alec to his feet. Pivoting, Galeric shoves the boy at his men.

Two Arkonai catch Alec, spin him around again to face Jackson, and hold him fast.

"All right, Saroth, I'm ready to hear you out, but if I don't like what you have to say, your apprentice will have a very long, painful night." He pauses to give the threat time to reach Jackson. "Do we understand each other?"

"As you say," Jackson replies.

I'm more than ready to leave Galeric's mind. Being this near to pure evil saps spiritual strength, but I force myself to stay for Vic's sake. Jackson's been ignoring her of late. That is worrisome, for a delay means that the plan he's working through must be elaborate.

When Galeric moves into range, Jackson reads a simple privacy spell from a small scroll he conjures. The use of magic repulses Galeric, but he confines the distaste to a sneer. Despite possessing Seeker Gifts, Galeric has long prided himself on not needing magic.

The two men exchange long, measuring looks.

"What is it you could not share with my men?" Galeric asks.

"I know you've been destroying Saroth everywhere you encounter them," says Jackson. "While this is good, I'd like to help you find certain targets if you'll agree to turn them over to me."

"You want to hire me?" Galeric's statement contains three-quarters disbelief and a quarter of a question.

"Yes. You've attracted people who can control those whose reach extends beyond the Veil. If we're to win the fight against the Darkland creatures, I need access to certain Saroth who may be reluctant to help."

On the surface, what Jackson says makes sense, but I know his heart enough to sense the lie. There are grains of truth within the lie, but I'm not certain which part. Jackson's largely responsible for there being a Darkland army amassing in the Ashlands, but logic says he will one day have to destroy that army once it has served its purpose and subdued the land. The easiest way to control the Darkland army would be to use Victoria, but Jackson has not had much luck controlling her.

"Which ones? And what do I gain from this arrangement?" Galeric wonders.

"I will pay a bounty for each target on this list." Jackson waves and a sealed scroll flies out of the Veil and into his outstretched hand. "Do not look at it until you're ready to accept the assignment. You're actually on the trail of several targets now, but there's a certain order they should be captured in. Those details are contained in the contract along with tips for anticipating their movements."

"Where did you get that?" hisses Galeric. He narrows his eyes at the seal on the scroll.

The seal belongs to Supreme Huntmaster Jordan Lekros.

"Our master has servants on both sides of this conflict," Jackson states. "Let us concentrate on our mutual enemies for the moment. When the Darkland crisis passes, you'll be free to continue your holy war against my people to your heart's content."

"Why would you use your people then betray them?" wonders Galeric.

A cold smile comes easily to Jackson.

"The same reason you're willing to murder your people," he replies. "They deserve it."

"I execute traitors," Galeric says flatly. "Those who sympathize with Saroth. If I take this contract, how will I explain it to my men?"

"I'm making your job easier," Jackson points out. "I will tell you who to locate and where to find them. Your Supreme Huntmaster will soon supply the means of reaching the far-flung targets. I'll leave the selection of your strike force up to you."

"How many men will I need? What skills will they need? And what will I do with the rest of the men?" Galeric fires the questions in rapid succession.

"Each target will require a hand-picked team, but for the first few, continue on as one group," Jackson advises. "When you have them all, meet me at the Alamon Temple. I'll deliver the rest of your payment for the first targets at that time, but until then, this should show you what sort of riches you can earn here."

Jackson snaps his fingers and conjures a small, heavy bag. It lands at Galeric's feet with a thud. The leather tie woven into the top loosens enough for several gold coins to spill out. I'm surprised at the amount of wealth being displayed. Where is the money coming from? The Castaloni holdings in the east have always done well, but Jackson must have a different source. Someone would protest if he was spending that much on a private war.

"Do we have a deal?"

Galeric's eyes lock on the money. He'll agree. He might bluster, but his heart's hooked on the wealth. Such riches could fund an army many times larger than the one that follows him now. His mind fills with visions of whole cities answering his glorious call to battle. In his head, he's already a legend.

"We do," Galeric answers.

"Excellent." Another snap of Jackson's fingers breaks the privacy spell.

Murmurs from the men reach Jackson and Galeric. The Resolute leader signals his men who promptly release Alec. The boy rushes forward to join Jackson.

I eagerly return to Alec and wait for Jackson to take us back to Fort Medron. My soul is uneasy. The Outcast has arrayed very strange allies. In a way, Jackson's just accomplished what Victoria seeks to do. He's arranged for Arkonai and Saroth to work side by side toward one goal. I would be encouraged except that I believe his one goal is destroying my young Chosen Redeemer. With my grace and that of the One resting upon her, that will be difficult for him, but it's not impossible.

Chapter 12:
Forest Battle

Katrina Polani
Silver Springs Forest

After setting our traps, Tellen and I spend the last few pre-battle moments arguing. He's determined to use every weapon at his disposal, including lightning bolts, arrows, and daggers. I'm trying to talk sense into him.

"If the traps fail, we'll likely be captured," I remind him. "Should that happen, there's a small chance you can convince them this is my doing."

"They'll never believe me," he argues. "Besides, if we fully fight, we stand a better chance of not being captured or killed."

"I'm not saying we don't fight," I snap. "I'm saying we fight smart. You can't fight them like an Arkonai. Don't let them know you're responsible for the traps."

We're prevented from entering round six of the same arguments when a man screams in pain. The accompanying sharp crack tells me it's one of Tellen's creations.

My early scouting in beetle form indicates that there are twenty-two Resolute Arkonai and at least a hundred Bereft followers. I mentally subtract one. Even if the man's alive, he probably won't walk for a few days.

We've rigged a variety of surprises for our foes. Some, like the one just discovered, are spring traps triggered by the victim stepping in a particular spot. Others are time-delayed bolts of lightning scattered about. These I approve of. What I've warned Tellen against is direct lightning strikes. The traps can be blamed on unseen others, even me, depending on how knowledgeable these Arkonai are about my people. Still others must be set off manually. That part will be tricky.

I spend much of the battle slithering from one fire trap to another, briefly switching to human form long enough to light them before moving on.

As the fires spread, the number of panicked screams increases. Men cough and choke and curse the smoke filling the air. They fire arrows aimlessly and thrash at the branches with their swords. The horses ridden by the Resolute buck and scream along with the men. Three Bereft start to retreat. One of the Resolute maneuvers his horse to block their escape. He points a gun at the men and shouts something I can't make out. A Bereft man tries to duck past the horse, but he flies back into a tree when the rider urges the horse to kick him. The others shrink away from the horse and the angry man, but neither do they turn to press on into the woods.

Similar scenes repeat themselves all over the Silver Springs Forest. More Bereft men perish by the hands of their commanders trying to control them than those that fall victim to our traps. I continue to set fires and occasionally use snake form to trip our enemies.

Fires rage nearly everywhere now. The crackling snaps and pops of hungry flames provides a steady backdrop to the noise of battle. Several men fight each other, adding the clang of swords to the mix.

Despite the early confusion, the Arkonai soon organize the men. They collectively press on through the forest.

I lost track of Tellen early, but now I see him weaving through the trees, coming toward me.

"Katrina! Katrina! Where are you?" he calls. He's in such a hurry he rushes right past my hiding spot.

I'm not sure how he senses he's gone too far but he stops and looks around frantically.

"Here," I say, reverting to human form. Reaching out, I pull him down to a sheltered depression where we can hide a moment. We land on our sides facing each other. "What is it?"

"We must stop the fires!" he cries. Tellen's eyes glitter with grief and conviction. His hands are clenched into fists. "They've brought women and children into the woods. Slaves, I think, but regardless, we can't kill them. It would be murder."

Seeing his concern melts something in me. Nodding, I close my eyes, fold my hands over my heart, and concentrate on sensing where the flames are located. Silently spreading my spirit throughout the forest takes a lot of effort, but at last, I believe I know where each fire burns. Having the power to cause fire also means having the ability to snuff it out. I've never done it on this scale before, but the principle is the same as holding fire in the palm of one's hand.

The flames and screams die away.

Quiet reigns for a short time before the men start murmuring about witchcraft. In the distance, I hear a child's sobs. Sounds of men moving come from every direction. I don't need animal senses to know we're surrounded.

I remove my hands from my chest and reach out to Tellen.

Grabbing hold of my hands, Tellen whispers.

"Get out of here! Tell Vic and Sara we fought well."

I could leave. It would be a simple matter of taking on beetle form and flying away. The Resolute might suspect something, but they'd never catch me. Yet I can't leave. If I do, they will capture Tellen and execute him. There's only one chance he has of living.

I suddenly realize I love him. With our people on the brink of war and the world besieged by Darkland creatures, there's no point in it, but hearts never made much sense.

"There's no reason both of us should die," he hisses. "You can fly away."

"Give me your dagger," I say.

"Why?" Tellen squeezes my hands harder. One of his twin daggers leaves its sheath and floats up next to us.

"Do you trust me?" I search his eyes for answers.

"Of course, but—"

Using our clasped hands to bring him close, I cut him off with a kiss. I meant for the kiss to be a quick farewell, but his response is to pull me closer and let it linger. Finally, breaking it off, I quickly explain the facts to him along with part of a plan that's popped into my head.

"They'll want me alive, at least for a time. They'll kill you unless you can be their hero." I pluck the dagger from the air where it waits for us to finish our heart-to-heart. Tucking the handle into Tellen's hand, I aim it toward my chest.

He pushes himself up with his left arm, protest etched into every feature.

"Katrina, I can't do this! Please. I'd rather let them kill me."

"Don't give up just yet," I urge.

"Halt! What's going on here?" calls a male voice from behind

Tellen.

"Sell them the story or we both die," I whisper. "You can free me later using the baydonberries."

"Why are your plans always crazy?" he murmurs. His expression shifts from heartbroken and conflicted to calm and aloof. He grips the dagger's handle tighter and brings the blade to my neck, tilting my head back.

"I've come across a prize I think Huntmaster Galeric would like to see," Tellen says coolly.

The man comes closer and whistles when he gets a better look at me.

"Let me help you with that," offers the man. His clothes bear scorch marks where he narrowly escaped the flames.

A small crowd gathers around us, including several slaves. The Bereft man reaches into his pocket and withdraws a large key. Quickly, he crosses to one of the slaves and unlocks the shackles binding her wrists and neck. I've heard of such restraining devices before but never dreamed I'd see—or experience—them.

Tellen cautiously climbs to his feet and lets the man approach.

I fight the instinct to turn into a dog and bite the Bereft man. Instead, I do nothing. The warm metal bindings fasten around my wrists. I twist my head away from the metal piece he tries to slip around my neck, but I don't have much room to move.

"There's nowhere to go, sweetheart," says the Bereft man. When his task is done, he hauls me to my feet.

Drawing himself up, Tellen comes to my side and pushes the man away.

"I want to see Huntmaster Galeric," says Tellen.

"What reason do you have to see me?" asks a different male voice. This one has the ring of command and arrogance I've come to expect from the Resolute Arkonai. He slowly enters the small clearing on a large, black horse. His blond hair rivals mine for length and is tied back in a manner that forms a tail high on his head. A pair of guns hang from leather holders that crisscross his chest. "Who are you?"

"That's Tellen, son of Huntmaster Callen," offers a third man. This one too rides a horse. "I don't know his loyalties but his father's a Saroth sympathizer."

"What say you, boy? Are you a traitor?" asks the leader.

"I follow my own heart," Tellen replies. "I'm here to join you."

"This is an unusual place for a convert to seek us out," notes

Galeric. "When did you see the light?"

"I've always believed. I've just not had the opportunity to seek out likeminded Resolute before," Tellen explains. "As Huntsman Tanner mentioned, my father does not share our beliefs."

"Prove it," barks Galeric. He motions and several men obey the silent commands.

A pair of men shoo Tellen off a step and take hold of my arms. Soon, I'm kneeling between Galeric's horse and my friend.

"I'm assuming this is the Saroth responsible for the trouble my men experienced in these woods," says Galeric in a conversational tone. "That deserves punishment."

He motions again and one of the followers tosses him a staff. Catching it, Galeric twirls the long rod twice before pitching it toward Tellen.

"Beat her with that," he orders.

My heart thuds in my chest. I don't dare look at Tellen for fear I'll destroy the deception.

"No."

The word strikes a new chord of fear within me. I don't have to look to see the gathered men shifting, anticipating an order to fight Tellen.

"No?" Galeric repeats, stunned at the refusal.

"I refuse to beat a prisoner," Tellen explains. "It's beneath me."

Galeric draws up next to Tellen and holds his hand out for the staff. When it's in his hand he whips it around and down until it connects with Tellen's left shoulder, knocking him to his knees.

I close my eyes and bite back a cry. I want to go to him, but I cannot show that I care.

"Never lecture me, and never question my orders. Do you understand?" Galeric's voice is low and full of malice.

"I do," Tellen says solemnly.

"Good. Then, put your prisoner with the other slaves. I'll decide her fate later."

"I wouldn't do that," says the last voice I'd ever expect to hear in this forest.

My head jerks up, and I spot Jackson Castaloni standing in the midst of the Bereft followers. They shrink away from him so fast his black cloak rustles.

"Don't you fools know a Shapeshifter when you see one?" asks Vic's uncle. The Conjurer looks unimpressed with the dozens of weapons leveled his way, including both of Galeric's guns.

"What do you want, Saroth?" Galeric spits the question out like it tastes bad.

"I want to keep you from making a grave mistake," answers Jackson in his oily, creepy voice. My heart sinks when he points to me. "That girl is Katrina Polani, daughter of Marcus Polani, a man with a lot of influence with the Tariku League. You'd do well to keep her safe. Besides, she's one of the targets I asked you to look for, as is the boy." His tone has a *must-I-do-everything-myself* quality to it.

"How was I supposed to know that?" Galeric whines. He shoves his guns into their holders. "It's not like she shapeshifted in front of us, and they're not exactly traveling with a kid like you said they would."

"Never mind that," says Jackson. "Now that you know, keep them contained until I need them. Here. Put this on the girl, it will prevent her from using her Gift, and remember that the boy can access lightning at will." He tosses Galeric a thin, leather collar studded with tiny, clear crystals.

"If the girl's a Shapeshifter, why is she still here?" Huntsman Tanner wonders. "She had plenty of chances to slip away."

Jackson laughs.

"She cares for the boy, of course." He waves toward Tellen. "Feel free to use that connection against them. It may prove better control than all the bindings you can muster."

Dozens of hands fall upon Tellen, binding his wrists behind him and wrapping ropes around his arms. They pick him up and drop him to his knees in front of me. We exchange sad looks.

Climbing down from his horse, Galeric throws the collar to Huntsman Tanner and approaches us. Next, he draws a gun again and presses it to the back of Tellen's head.

"All right, girl. Tanner's going to release the neck piece of your current bindings and apply the new one. I suggest you keep very still while he works, or the boy will suffer."

"I need them alive," Jackson reminds Galeric.

Somehow the words don't comfort me. I can't imagine what Jackson wants us for, but his schemes have already caused untold amounts of trouble. He is Saroth, but if he intends to use me against the Tariku League, he truly does not know our people. My fear is that he'll find a way to leverage us against Vic.

Chapter 13:
Plains Battle

Victoria Saveron
Path to the Alamon Temple, Plains of Forgiveness
We're not going to make it to the Dancing Woods Forest. Soon into our desperate flight and just before I sent her to check on the Piccards, Sara told me of Tellen's instruction to seek the Arkonai huntsman assigned to protect the forest. I'd been looking forward to having a fully capable fighter with us. Hope of that possibility disappears when the scout I'd sent ahead—Tomeo Valor—comes charging back. The young man's skin rivals his black stallion's in color. Both are breathing hard.

"Zombies ahead! We must go back!" he shouts.

Ryle Ezard looks to me and I nod. We'd discussed this scenario at length over the last few hours of hard marching.

"Thank you, Tomeo. Warn the other riders then join the reserves," Ryle says.

The column halts behind us.

I try to catch Ryle's eye, but he's carefully avoiding my gaze.

"Ryle." I reach out and touch the big man's left arm.

"I should go with you," he says, clenching his hands into fists.

"If I fail, the people will need you," I whisper, trying not to let my words carry to the villagers waiting a respectful distance behind us.

"Don't say that!" Ryle shouts. He squeezes his eyes shut for a second before finally looking at me. "Please. At least take my sword." Drawing the beautiful blade out of its scabbard, Ryle turns the blade downward and angles it back to present the weapon to me handle-first.

Compelled to accept the blade, I grip the handle, a little surprised

65

by the weight of the weapon. The steel blade is cool against the fingertips of my good hand.

I smile and hold the handle up between us until he grips it.

"Thank you, but I wouldn't know the first thing about wielding such a weapon."

"What will you fight with?" Ryle asks. He returns the sword to its home.

"I'll know when I get there," I answer. My bracers snap out to their defensive positions and light up. "Keep the people back. Have Torin and Joshua keep an eye on the main force, and see if you can lead the people far enough south to swing around our enemies."

Sara rushes up, having sprinted from the position I'd assigned her well back in the column of refugees. Her cheeks are flushed and her eyes flash with anger. She knows why I sent her back to check on Nina and Roman Piccard. She steps up to come with me, but Ryle catches hold of her shoulders.

I wish I had time to explain myself properly, but I spin away and dash up the slight hill blocking our view of the Darkland horde. My willingness to face danger doesn't cover tears. Sara's expression mixes anguish and betrayal, and it rips at my heart, driving me to run faster.

I'm sorry, Sara, but you cannot follow this part of my path.

As I top the crest of the hill, I look down and see a sea of zombies and other Darkland creatures slowly marching toward me.

The scouts got a few things right, but they were dead wrong on the number of foes. This force stretches for miles. There must be nearly a thousand enemies if not more, and there are indeed several kitsarue and Denkari spread throughout the force. The zombie moans combine with hacking coughs, low growls, and an occasional howl, creating an eerie symphony.

Aware of another presence drawing up beside me, I look over and see Torin standing next to me with his bow ready for action. Ten more archers fan out to the left of him.

Ten against a thousand is impossible odds. Even the sixty fighters we could muster from the village would barely slow this gathering.

"If it comes down to a fight, aim for the normal zombies," I instruct my unwanted help. "And stay here." Lacking time to send them away, I jog down the hill still without much of a plan.

"Vic. Stop." The voice that fills my entire being is the same strong yet tender masculine voice I first heard in Fort Amareth.

I skid to a stop at the bottom of the hill, and the horde in front of me halts too.

"Use your Gift, dear daughter. Let my armies protect you."

"Papa." I whisper the word with surprise. Sara must be rubbing off on me. Hearing no more words, I continue pouring out my heart to the One. "I don't know what to do. I don't want to lose any of them." I look up into the empty sky then realize how foolish that is and close my eyes and bow my head. "I am yours to command, but I lack the wisdom to be of much use. Be my guiding light, my source of strength, and my peace in this moment."

My eyes open in time to see one of the Denkari snarl and bark a command at the forces around him. They start advancing again.

Heart trembling, I feel doubt creep in.

"Vic. Trust me. I have given you their lives this day. You will have what you need when you need it."

The words root me in place. Raising both hands in a stopping gesture, I close my eyes, half-expecting a zombie archer to send an arrow through me.

"Hama, serloahta Kailon, merchail etparata esserco onpapa declospria. Taportos arestio halna mitro kelsalvo." In the common language, the words mean, "Hear me, servants of the Eternal King, step forth and protect these which our Father has called precious. The gates holding you back have no power while He wills it so."

As I finish speaking, my hands go rigid until I open my eyes and force myself to relax. Tremendous power fills me from the top of my head down to the soles of my feet. I feel like I've stepped close to a raging fire.

Spreading my hands wide, I channel the energy into a spot about ten feet in front of me. Both spots where the energy strikes form pools of blue-white light. With quick gestures, I raise both incomplete portals upright and move them away from each other. The energy coursing through me does not relent. I fashion two more portals and likewise move them aside to make room for more. This process repeats again until there are six portals arrayed before me, and still, more energy flows. This time, I move my hands close together and concentrate on the last portal.

My personal energy levels drop dangerously, but I can't afford to collapse right now.

A wall of arrows flies up from a line of zombie archers moving up behind the main force. For two seconds I watch the arrows rise gracefully, but the deadly rain quickly closes in on its target: the small gathering of archers on the hill behind me causing many cries of dismay.

At the last moment, I raise my hands high above my head and spread my arms in a wide arc that brings my hands down to my sides. Light flows up from my bracers and spreads into a tent above us, catching every arrow and directing it down to the ground away from flesh and blood.

The battle gets messy from there.

When my shocked companions recover their senses, they unleash their own arrows at our enemies. Once again, I raise my hands and close my eyes. I feel each arrow in flight and pray for it to multiply. As the arrows rise, each doubles then triples. The scores of arrows I directed into the ground near the archers behind me rise up of their own accord and join the other arrows headed toward the enemy. Upon nearing the enemy, every arrow doubles and triples again, each headed for a different target. The hail of arrows descends like a curtain, taking out a good bit of the attacking force. The remaining zombies scream defiantly and quicken their pace. The kitsarue race ahead of the main force and crash headlong into the first warriors to step through the seven portals I've created.

Teeth snap and sharp claws reach for the ethereal fighters but my supernatural help meets the challenge with spirit blades that gleam with holy light. I don't have much time to watch the battle, but at one point, I see the commander of Kailon's army—shown by the red cape he wears over his white robes—level his sword at a particularly large kitsarue. A bolt of lightning shoots from the sword and throws back the attacker, casting the beast into three zombies. They crumble to dust.

My bracers form long, thin spikes that extend an arm's length beyond my hands. I cross the blades over my head in time to catch a hard strike from a Denkari's sword. He strikes four more times in quick succession, but each time, one of the spikes intercepts the blow. Shrieking, the Denkari levels a devastating mental blow in my direction. I can tell because three men behind me collapse under the weight of the assault. The attack feels like increasing pressure upon my head, but the mental defense the One has granted me holds.

While the Denkari is slightly distracted, I stab him in the chest with one of my bracer spikes. Black smoke gushes out of the wound, and the Denkari's screech changes pitch. The spirit warrior recoils and regards me with shock and contempt. It spits a dark liquid at me, but I duck under the stream. The grass where the liquid strikes smokes and blackens. The Denkari hisses at me.

"Your master cannot always protect you, little one," he says, holding a hand over his wound. "We can wait and destroy you later." With that promise, the Denkari withdraws.

That moment becomes a turning point. Our enemies slowly lose the will to fight. One by one, the other Denkari and the kitsarue finish their current contests and retreat. The regular zombies continue to press the attack, but the white-robed army handles them with ease. I help by catching arrows aimed at my archers. Occasionally, I fling an arrow back at one of the zombies.

The air is thick with unholy dust from the vanquished zombies.

A scream rings out behind me, piercing my soul.

I know that voice.

Whirling, I will myself to Sara's side in time to destroy the zombie that's bitten her high on the left shoulder. My bracers retract the spikes in time to avoid stabbing Sara. I awkwardly catch her and ease her to the ground.

My heart feels like it's going to shatter. The little battles around me cease to matter. Three warriors in white approach and protect us, driving off a new wave of zombies.

I grasp Sara's right hand and squeeze hard. Her eyes had been closed in pain, but she opens them and focuses on me.

"What are you doing here?" I ask in a broken whisper. My vision blurs with tears.

"I came to help ye," Sara says, "and to witness this grand moment." The effort to speak drains her energy. She lays her head back.

If she begins to turn, I'll have to kill her or risk the lives of the villagers. The thought rips all others from my mind and my soul takes up a wordless keening plea on her behalf.

"Stretch forth your hands and touch the wound. It is not yet her time. I have granted you their lives this day."

I obey and press both hands over the large wound on Sara's shoulder. Light bursts from my bracers drawing a gasp from Sara. I don't see the wound close, but I feel the power leaving me as the One works through me. By the time the healing completes, I realize most of the villagers have gathered on the hill beside us.

The white-robed soldiers look on solemnly.

"Bring forth the others with wounds," orders the commander of the Army of Light.

At first, the villagers simply stare in disbelief, but eventually, they limp forward and present their battle wounds.

"When you finish here make haste to the temple," says the commander, addressing me. "The tide of darkness has turned but it will return. Be well, Chosen Redeemer."

When the situation is under control, the summoned army slips back through the portals. I watch them go, keenly aware of the One's gift to me. It's not likely to be repeated in the same way again.

Pushing aside the worry, I attend to what I can. Sword strikes, arrow wounds, and long gashes from kitsarue claws mar the flesh of many. Those who are more gravely injured are carried forth by friends and family. Sara's still weak, but she gets up and helps me tend the wounded. The light from my bracers is enough to drive off the disease and prevent the turning, but aside from Sara and perhaps one or two others, I cannot close the wounds. I heal the gravest, life-threatening injuries, but when I try to heal less severe ones, nothing happens.

Afterwards, the villagers converse in hushed tones around us, but mostly they avoid Sara and me. The battle has completely unnerved them. From the way they're looking at me, I know I'm going to have to say something eventually or they'll make me an idol in their hearts.

How can I explain what I don't understand?

I am only a child. The One and the Lady may have chosen to work through me, but that speaks more for their power than me. Sara could explain it better, but she's fallen asleep so I can't ask her about it. For now, the natural distance the villagers maintain will have to do.

Chapter 14:
The Observatory

The Lady
Polani Estate near the city of Jorash, Caramore

Adam Castillo fights the urge to take his wolf form and dash away. Ultimately, it is his decision to seek out his father and ask for help on Katrina's behalf. His mission to prepare the villagers for spiritual trouble and physical danger is largely at an end now, but there is always more to do. He's been waiting in this room for at least ten minutes and has still not removed the hood of his cloak nor taken the seat the servant gestured to.

Marcus Polani is three floors above him carefully considering the request for an audience. This could be a while. Marcus, the foremost spymaster in Caramore, has many reasons to fear for his life.

My thoughts drift to Daniel Saveron and Shadow. They have begun their journey to the Alamon Temple, but it is slow going for many reasons. For one thing, village portals are being destroyed or redirected into traps. Thus, Daniel and Shadow have been asked by the Arkonai High Council to investigate the state of each portal along the way. If they use Shadow's Gift, they risk drawing danger down upon them, for every strong use of magic leaves a traceable mark upon the world. Skilled Seekers and Minders can follow these marks with ease. In addition, the portal directly into the temple has been inactivated to prevent against an invasion from within. The closest they will be able to port is the city of Fortitude. I check on them often but there is precious little I can do to aid them.

A door opens and Marcus steps through followed by four

personal bodyguards. Adam keeps his head angled downward, hiding his features.

"Did my servant not offer to take your cloak, stranger?" Marcus inquires. He knows for a fact that the man indeed offered to take the cloak and was rebuffed.

"He did," Adam confirms, "but I have my reasons for declining the hospitality."

"State your business then," Marcus prompts.

"My business is for your ears alone," Adam responds. "Send these others away, and I will reveal myself."

Silence falls and Marcus considers the proposal. Few assassins would be bold enough to walk into his home, but a well-developed sense of caution has kept him alive this long.

"Would you consent to a confining spell?" Marcus asks.

"It would be a waste, but yes, I would," says Adam without hesitation. A confining spell would create four magical barriers to pen Adam in place until Marcus releases him. It's one of the few spells that cannot be forced upon another without delving deep into the dark arts. Having one on a scroll is outlawed in many places. Marcus has special permission from the Tariku League to carry one.

I can tell Marcus is intrigued by the way he studies Adam. He fires off several questions with easy answers to get a feel for his honesty. It's not a perfect system, but in this instance, Adam has nothing to hide. Deciding to trust him, Marcus motions for the guards to exit. The guard commander appears frustrated, but he salutes and obeys his master.

As the door closes, Adam whips off his hood. Marcus draws in a sharp breath. Young Adam's dark hair, striking blue eyes, and facial features strongly reflect those of the older man.

"What do you want?" Marcus asks hoarsely. Though he carefully controls his expression, I hear the buzzing of his surface thoughts. Just before her death, Gabriella—Marcus's wife—had revealed that Katrina had a twin, but she'd offered no details that would allow him to find the boy. This is the first time Marcus has laid eyes on his son.

It's not exactly a warm welcome, but Adam has no delusions of being received well. A man of Marcus's position has many people seeking his favor and advice. Keeping people at a distance is a natural form of emotional self-defense.

"Your aid, sire," says Adam. "Your daughter—my sister—is in grave danger."

"How do you know that?" Marcus's suspicions are clear, but I also hear worry in the question. "I don't even know where she is right now."

"That is a long tale, but with your permission, I will be brief." Once he receives Marcus's approval, Adam gives a very short summary of his connection to me then speaks of the recent events. He describes watching over Victoria, Katrina, and Tellen on their travels to Coldhaven and following them to Fort Amareth. "After the events in the fort, the Lady sent me to warn more villages. The Chosen Redeemer and her companions were to head to the Alamon Temple to request entry into Caramore. They did not make it."

"Travel has become difficult, perhaps they are simply delayed," Marcus points out.

Adam shakes his head firmly.

"It's more than that. The Lady will not tell me much, but she revealed that the party was split up. Katrina and the Arkonai boy called Tellen have fallen into the hands of dangerous men. They are somewhere between the Silver Springs Forest and the Alamon Temple."

I did not tell Adam more details because I currently have nothing to add. Galeric will probably heed Jackson's orders to safeguard Tellen and Katrina, but I've not kept a close watch on their situation. My powers have distinct limits in this realm.

"Why come to me?" Marcus is not looking for validation. He's not certain how he can help. Though he has access to many resources, he cannot simply redirect them at will for personal reasons.

"You must prepare the Tariku League to hear from Victoria," says Adam. "Ask them to rescue Katrina. She and the Lady's Chosen Redeemer will tell you how to fight the darkness seeping into the world."

Marcus hides his frustration well, but I can sense it. His surface thoughts churn with the possibilities. One of his enemies may have sent Adam with a false message. But if it's true, he needs to act. There's only one sure way to know, though it requires help from his people in Dominance. Even if justified, his enemies will have much to say. In the end, concern for his daughter prompts him to action.

"Put your hood up and come with me," Marcus says at last.

Expecting this, Adam obeys. The trip to Dominance would take many days if they had to walk or ride, but Marcus has connections in high places. In a matter of minutes, he works through several Minders to get a request through to the Academy of Arts and Sciences which also houses the office of Magical Defense where he works. Soon, Dante comes to retrieve them.

Dante Aurelius is a well-kept secret even among the highest government officials in Caramore. He's one of three Specters, a special form of Minder with the ability to teleport at will. His Gifts are different than Portal Masters or Gatekeepers. He cannot create portals, but he can move through the Veil at will and bring a few others with him. In this case, he appears in the room with Adam Castillo and Marcus Polani and takes up a position between them. Then, he simply grasps both of their wrists and whisks them to a pre-determined room within the Academy located in the heart of Dominance.

Having been warned by Marcus, Adam stays absolutely still. Dante drops his hand and scuttles away. Four spearmen level their long weapons at Adam. Several steps beyond them three archers line up shots and farther still two Destroyers cradle lightning between their hands. The large room seems quite crowded.

"I'll vouch for him," says Marcus.

"What's your hurry, Spymaster?" inquires a languid male voice. The tone adds a sarcastic edge to the title.

Marcus's frustration increases. He silently curses his luck. The duty of overseeing the comings and goings within this screening room is split among six Minders, most of whom Marcus gets along with very well. Emilio Jekar, however, lost the position of Spymaster to Marcus by a narrow margin when the political winds shifted against him due to an ill-timed scandal.

"We need to get to the Observatory to investigate a matter." Marcus lifts his chin imperiously.

"You can't take a stranger there," protests Emilio.

"I can do what I like," Marcus retorts. Though true to an extent, Marcus knows every word of this conversation will get back to the Tariku League eventually. He needs to tread with care.

"I will remain here if I must," Adam offers. "I trust you will know what to do when you see the situation for yourself."

"I may need your help," Marcus points out. He is loath to leave his son with Emilio. There's no telling what the man might do when he discovers Adam's identity. The moment is inevitable, but the longer Marcus can delay it, the better. Stepping forward and raising his voice, Marcus declares, "I will take full responsibility for this man within these walls."

Emilio narrows his eyes, but he understands that the most he can do is delay Marcus for a short while. Shrugging like he doesn't care, he waves dismissively and the spearmen lift their weapons away from Adam and slam the ends against the ground, making a sharp salute.

Thus released, Marcus quickly leads Adam to the Observatory. Contrary to its name, the Observatory is no tower. Instead, it's a room deep within the Academy that very few can access. Here, every moment of every day there are several Minders at work scanning for magical dangers and watching over the various territories that fall under Saroth control.

"Greetings, Master Marcus. What can I do for you?" asks Navina.

"I need to see something," says Marcus. "Is there an isolation chamber free?"

"Of course," replies Navina, picking up on his serious tone. "Right this way."

After dismissing the young Minder on duty in Isolation Chamber 3, Navina Christol ushers Adam and Marcus into the private room and activates the sound barriers that will keep their conversation private. Kneeling on the soft cushion in the center, Navina folds her hands in her lap and waits for one of them to deliver the request.

Adam misses the first cue from Marcus because he's too absorbed with taking in the setup. Isolation Chamber 3 is lit by three orbs of soft white light that circle the room near the ceiling. Several cushions like the one Navina occupies are arranged in a semi-circle behind the central cushion. The wall in front of them is blank, waiting for a Minder to cast his or her vision. A simple set of shelves off to the right side holds a collection of focusing crystals and other trinkets the Minders can use to concentrate their Gifts. Vision Casting is mentally draining work, but very rewarding for people in Marcus's profession. He doesn't do it much anymore, but he used to be quite talented at it.

A swift analysis of the comfortable interaction between Navina and Marcus tells me he trusts her. I bid Adam to tell his story.

"Where should I start the search?" Navina asks, once she grasps the situation.

"Start with the Plains of Forgiveness and move southeast toward the Alamon Temple," Adam instructs.

Navina draws a deep relaxing breath and waves for Marcus and Adam to be seated to either side of her. She's still kneeling on the cushion even though it's been several minutes. Summoning five focusing crystals from the shelves, Navina slowly directs them to positions along the far wall. The crystals form a loose circle connected to each other by thin tendrils of energy. Not satisfied with the pentagon that forms,

Navina adds another crystal, crafting a hexagon with the two longest sides in the middle.

At first, the surface remains blank, but soon, the energy from the edges bleeds toward the center where it meets and coalesces into a thin, white screen. Navina spends several seconds scanning the vast Plains of Forgiveness. The view they receive is similar to that of a hawk in flight until she spots the large encampment with its many fires and focuses her attention there. She gasps but holds out both hands to maintain the Vision Cast.

The sight makes Adam and Marcus cold with rage. Katrina stands in a makeshift dirt ring created by a temporary fence. Swords and spikes are placed at strategic locations to discourage escape attempts. She's surrounded by a crowd of rowdy men placing bets. On the opposite side, two men struggle to hold the ropes tied around the neck of a half-starved, mangy dog.

Chapter 15:
Ring Fight

Katrina Polani
Resolute Camp, Plains of Forgiveness
My faith in humanity slips a little more each day. The march through the Silver Springs Forest went fine, despite the weight of chains and ropes. Jackson Castaloni's instructions to Galeric earned both Tellen and I central positions within the column. The first day of travel was long and hard but pleasant compared to the recent days. The men grow more comfortable with our presence and their small cruelties have escalated. Missing an occasional meal and having to sleep in chains are tolerable, even understandable forms of abuse, but I have no words to depict this level of wrong.

They want me to fight for their entertainment.

Galeric used the possibility to spur them on at a rapid pace and cut down on complaints these last two days. He's up on a platform he made the men build for him. Tellen's there too, looking ill at ease. Several archers perch from wagons positioned with clear lines of sight to me and the vicious dog two men hold back on the far side.

I feel bad for the beast. Beneath the dirt and dried blood from previous fights, the large shepherd has a beautiful thick coat of brown and black fur. He's obviously malnourished and crazed with rage born of daily physical abuse. I don't want to hurt him, but if I fail to give the men a good fight, they will take their frustration out on Tellen. It's happened before. Yesterday, when I refused to shapeshift for Galeric, he ordered two men to beat Tellen with long cane rods. I eventually obeyed, but he had my love struck twice anyway. He enjoys pretending to be kind when he bids my guards to remove the collar that prevents me from shapeshifting.

I consider pleading but Galeric would never hear my words above this crowd. They place bets on how long the fight will last and what sorts of wounds will be dealt. Some say the beast will strike me first while others place their faith—and their money—on me. My mind screams incoherent prayers, and my heart feels like it will be crushed within me.

At Galeric's signal the men holding the dog back release the ropes. The beast springs forward and crashes hard into the boards behind me. It would have pinned me there and made short work of me had I stayed in human form, but I take snake form and slip under his attack. They have forbidden me from using beetle form tonight. My dog form might fare okay even though I am slighter than my opponent, but I prefer the quicker reflexes of this form.

The men watching the fight erupt with cheers and shouts of dismay. Shaking itself, the shepherd recovers his feet, whirls, and charges again. I dodge left, earning a round of jeers and curses. We do a few more rounds of this dance with the dog charging and me dodging, causing him to repeatedly slam his body up against the wooden boards they've penned us in with. I take care not to dodge in front of the few sections where swords and spears poke through the ring, but the crowd is growing restless with my tactics.

After drawing the dog into one more fruitless charge, I streak to the opposite end of the ring and revert to human form. This time, I wait in a kneeling position. When he closes the distance, I snap my fingers and cast two small fireballs at his feet. Squealing with fright, the dog abruptly skids to avoid the flames. The men argue over the legality of my move, increasing the noise level tenfold. Before they can render a ruling, I set off more mini-fireballs near the dog in quick order, alternating sides until he trips over one of the trailing ropes. Seizing the loose end, I take to snake form again and weave in and out of the dog's legs, bringing the rope with me. In seconds, I've wrapped up my furious opponent.

The dog writhes and growls, trying to bite me, but I switch to dog form and bark at him, thoroughly confusing the poor beast into silence. Back in human form, I place my left hand on his head, lean close, and whisper words into his ears. He probably doesn't understand them, but he can gather from the cadence that I mean him no harm. After repeating the soothing phrases, I release the ropes entangling the beast's legs.

The men argue, and Galeric signals one of the archers. The man fires an arrow at the dog. Turning to snake form, I coil and spring at the last possible moment, knocking into the side of the arrow and throwing it off course. I turn back into a human upon hitting the makeshift fence they've built. Thankfully, I strike a section free of swords. The impact of my body loosens the boards. I land on my hands and knees, giving me an idea. Whistling sharply, I get the dog's attention and wave him over. If he misunderstands my signal, he will die.

Fortunately, the dog picks up on my intent perfectly. Racing forward at top speed, the big dog leaps at me. I form a shelf with my back and brace. Soon, the dog's up and over the barrier. The other archer fires an arrow but it sinks into one of the boards making up the barrier. He reaches for another arrow, and I set his whole quiver afire. He shrieks and flings the quiver away, spilling the arrows into the crowd. The men scream and dance away from the flames. I extinguish them almost immediately, but the panic blinds the crowd to the fact that they're in no danger. Men knock into each other and draw swords, ready to turn the mess into a proper brawl.

"Enough!" Galeric's shout causes movement to cease.

I watch the dog blaze a trail through the camp and wait until he's out of sight. Feeling every eye upon me, I slowly face Galeric. The ghost of a smile brightens Tellen's features, showing me he's proud of my decision, but I can take no joy in the victory for I know there will be a cost.

Nearly every man holds his sword or dagger in hand. Galeric stands atop his platform with a gun in hand. Frustrated, he swings the barrel at the side of Tellen's head. Tellen tries to dodge but he can only move so far since he's kneeling. The gun strikes a glancing blow, but Galeric quickly follows this with a kick that sends Tellen off the platform and into the ring with me. The ropes pinning his arms in place prevent him from bracing, but he rolls to absorb the impact. I'm by his side instantly and check his eyes to make sure they're focusing.

Around us, the men frantically tear down the barriers, leap up and over, and approach cautiously with swords leading the way.

Galeric waves for them to wait and they halt.

"You did well," Tellen whispers. "He's gone. Take heart in that." He has no time to say more because Galeric has men drag him away from me until several steps lie between us.

I study the trampled ground. Two men prop Tellen up between them and three others press swords to his sides and neck. The soil feels cold and unyielding. They can't harm him without arousing Jackson Castaloni's wrath, but they can—and will—hurt him for what I've done. I don't bother standing up.

Men murmur until Galeric silences them with a gesture. He knows he has to assert control quickly or risk losing their respect. Galeric allows the oppressive silence to linger to an uncomfortable point before slowly starting to clap. The motion and steady beat mocks us.

"Very entertaining, Saroth," he praises. A hard smile twists his features. It's not a pleasant expression and even that vanishes. "But I'm out a good fighting dog. Who's going to pay for that?"

Lacking patience for a verbal dance, I say nothing.

"Answer me!" Galeric demands.

Hands pull me up to a standing position. I do not fight them even though I long to.

"What would you like me to say?" I ask.

"Who should pay?" he repeats. Galeric's not talking about money.

"I should," I answer. My chin tilts up but that's the extent of my defiance.

"You should," he echoes darkly. "Your actions are undisciplined, disorderly, and destructive, things I cannot abide in my camp."

I spread my hands.

"So deliver your punishment and end this spectacle." A soul-deep weariness comes over me, and I lean heavily upon my captors.

At another gesture from Galeric, the men force me to kneel. Somebody pulls my hair aside, and the cold metal collar slips into place. My hands are not bound, but without the ability to shapeshift, the hands holding my arms are like iron shackles.

Tellen's trying to catch my eye, but I avoid his gaze. The question I read there asks if I'm ready to end this. Should I consent, he'll throw off the hands and destroy half this crowd with a devastating lightning assault. We will both die, but at least we'll go out fighting. I don't want that end for me and certainly not for Tellen, but I also don't want these men to die thus either. The notion surprises me because they've made it abundantly clear we are enemies.

I've heard it said that those in prolonged captivity can fall sway to their captors' charisma, but this is different. The change is not in them or because of them. It's in me. I see the emptiness in their eyes. There's a deadness like the one in zombies.

Two men escort me up the platform steps to stand in front of

Galeric. More men scramble over the platform making modifications, but I don't pay much attention to them. When I come within striking distance, Galeric brings the back of his right hand across my left cheek hard enough to snap my head back. The men holding my arms steady me, and Galeric's left fist crashes into my side, folding me in half. Almost tenderly, I'm lowered to my knees again. Galeric kneels with me and speaks low.

"I want to tell you a secret." A soft touch lifts my chin up. "I keep the contract with that Conjurer so he'll lead me to more of your kind, but a day is coming when I will break it and give you and that traitor the fate you both deserve. Until then, consider this a small taste of what's to come."

As he stands, he pulls me up by the hair and shoves me toward the men who have been working on the platform. They've cut a hole in the center and lowered a sturdy beam down into it. I think it once held up a large tent, but they've cut it down to a size that suits them. The rough beam digs into my back as my arms are tied behind me. A rope pulls tight around my neck, and I cannot look away. When I peer down into the ring, I see they've secured a large wooden beam across Tellen's shoulders. He stands alone in the center of the ring. The same two men who tormented him yesterday stand to either side. He faces me with a stoic expression. They've removed his shirt, and I can see the welts inflicted previously.

"Please, don't do this," I whisper. I am far beyond pride at this point.

"If he can stand three strikes without falling, I will count the punishment complete," says Galeric.

"And if he falls?" I ask.

"The count starts over."

Chapter 16:
Temple Troubles

Victoria Saveron
Tent Camp to Central Meeting Chamber, Alamon Temple

We are not the only refugees to seek safety at the Alamon Temple—one of the few neutral zones. Many villagers seek to wait out the war here. A large tent camp has formed below the temple. Guards wearing thick red cloaks maintain order while servants in plain brown robes scurry about trying to meet the people's needs. Nevertheless, I hear the murmured complaints and grumblings. There's not enough food, shelter, or water to sustain crowds this size for long. A solution springs up to each problem that reaches my ears, but I say nothing. The time has not yet come for me to speak. Lines stretch out of sight in every direction for even the most basic service. Tempers are short and fights are frequent.

Ryle Ezard leaves Caleb Anderson in charge of organizing the people of Sorrow Falls. Our account of the battle on the Plains of Forgiveness has earned us an audience with the Keris Council.

Along the last leg of our journey, Sara updated my knowledge about how the Alamon Temple is run. The ruling Council consists of seven members, including three lifetime positions that must be filled by a Saroth, an Arkonai, and a Bereft. The other four positions rotate more often. These belong to the Captain of the Temple Guards, the Keeper of Knowledge, the Keeper of the Grounds, and the scribe. Sara was most excited to tell me about the scribe. That position changes almost daily, and the person occupying the positon must be at least twelve. By tradition, the scribe often abstains from important votes, but he or she has an equal vote which reminds the other members that every opinion must be weighed.

My previous knowledge came from an old, dry book on religious orders. According to Sara, the Alamon Temple was started by the Keris monks, a sect of Saroth pacifists. They sought to retreat from the world and worship in peace. Eventually, Arkonai pilgrims lost their way traveling from Ardor to Temperance and decided to stay as well. Bereft scholars also found a home in the Temple, and word spread that anyone willing to earn their keep could find rest there. Over the years, it became an academy where the most skilled masters amongst both the Arkonai and the Saroth could find and train talented apprentices.

The temple itself is built into the side of Mount Arktur, the westernmost point of the Black Horn Mountains. The winding path leading up to the actual building starts out gentle but quickly steepens. I'm out of breath by the time we reach the imposing front gates. Even standing wide open, the red painted gates cause one to pause and reflect.

As I brush my fingers along one of the gates, a vision strikes me and I flinch. The picture shows fire engulfing these gates and people charging up the path we just climbed. Sara plucks my hand away from the door and pats it gently, tugging to prompt me to follow. We've fallen behind the others. She doesn't know what I've seen, but my expression tells her I saw something unpleasant. I know she wants to hear of it, but now is not the right time for me to share the vision. Twisting my head around, I look back at the tent camp, planting my feet enough to bring Sara to a halt. Day eases into night and new campfires spring up around the camp. It's beautiful. A lump forms in my throat when I think of the hundreds of souls down there. Sara lets me linger a few seconds before gently pulling on my arm again.

"Come now, we've a council waiting on us," Sara says.

I let her know the message is received, retrieve my hand, and wave for her to lead the way. Together, we jog to catch up to Ryle Ezard and Master Ori, the Keeper of Knowledge, who came to escort us to the meeting.

The Central Meeting Chamber is large but the cushions lined up along the front are arranged in a way that makes the conference seem close and personal. A single orb of energy hovering near the ceiling lends light to the place. There aren't enough cushions for us. Seeing this, a young boy sets aside the scroll cradled in his lap and retrieves another from a stack in the far corner. Master Ori handles introductions for both sides. The boy shyly setting a cushion in place for me is the scribe, Etienne. From left to right facing us are Captain Gerard Rillis, Keeper

Jemma Heston, an empty cushion for Master Ori, Shapeshifter Master Giovani Patros, Huntmaster Beatrice, David Hart, and Scribe Apprentice Etienne.

Ryle tells of New Haven's fate, the renaming ceremony, and the journey undertaken by the Sorrow Falls people. Next, Sara describes the recent clash with the Darkland creatures and testifies to the miracle of not having a single villager perish. The Keris Council members listen intently before fixing their attention on me. When it's my turn, they wave me forward into the light's center.

"What is it you seek, Chosen Redeemer?" asks Master Patros.

"We wish to go to Caramore to seek help from the Tariku League in the city of Dominance," I answer.

Master Patros's expression doesn't change.

"What do you think that will accomplish?" he asks.

"I do not know," I admit, "but I have to try. They must be warned that there are people actively sowing seeds of war. If we let that happen, the holes in the Veil will widen ever faster and Darkland creatures will continue to invade this land."

"Where does your knowledge come from, child?" asks Huntmaster Beatrice.

"The Lady, servant of Kailon," I answer, bracing for the usual reactions. People either believe me, which leads them to have greater faith and hope, or they think I'm lying. The latter type falls into two camps, those that think I'm crazy and those that think I'm mistaken. I'm interested to see how this council will divide itself over the issue, but before their debate moves too far, a young guard bursts in and halts just inside.

"Captain Rillis!" he calls. "Trouble's coming, sir!"

The Guard commander is on his feet in an instant. The rest of us follow quickly.

"Give your report, Damien," Captain Rillis orders calmly.

Before he can speak, another man appears and salutes. This one stands a respectful half-step behind the first, but he too is bursting with news.

"Stand fast, Killian. When Damien's done reporting, you can speak your mind," says Captain Rillis.

"One of the refugee hunters spotted a large force approaching from the plains to the west," Damien reports.

"What manner of force?" asks Captain Rillis.

"Bereft men, sir, but he thinks there may be Arkonai with them,"

Damien replies.

After dismissing Damien, Captain Rillis waves for Killian to share his news.

"Darkland forces are amassing on Mount Tangi. Minder Gera thinks they're coming here," says Killian.

"There's also a small party of Resolute huntsmen led by the Supreme Huntmaster approaching from the south," adds a female voice from behind Killian.

The young man steps left to make room for a stooped woman leaning heavily on a stick.

"Lady Gera, are you well?" asks Keeper Jemma. Without waiting for an answer, she dispatches the scribe for a cup of water.

"Mother, you shouldn't have walked this far," scolds Master Patros. Picking up the cushion he's been sitting on, he rushes over to the woman and settles her gently on top of it. He leans her against the door.

"I had to see her," whispers the lady. Despite these words, the woman leans heavily against the door and shuts her eyes in an effort to rally her strength.

Drawn to the woman, I kneel before her and pick up one of her frail hands. Her eyes focus on me, and a smile brightens her face. I brace my left hand on the upper part of her right arm and prepare to reach out and pour spirit strength into her. Until this moment, I didn't even know I could consciously do such a thing, but I'm used to discovering new aspects of my Gifts. There was a time when I thought the ability to light up when dark creatures approached would only get me killed. How little I knew. How little I still know.

As my thoughts connect with the woman, I close my eyes and see her within the blank space of my mind. This version of her stands upright and appears several decades younger, but I can see the same brightness within her that I sense in this woman I kneel before.

"Keep the grace given to you, dear one. I have lived a full life and only linger because I was promised I would see you before going to rest."

I open my eyes and remove my left hand. With great effort, the woman reaches out to Master Patros. Accepting the hand, he kneels on her other side and bows over the hand. I don't know what she's telling him, but he nods several times. Everybody watches solemnly. Lady Gera's breaths slow even further until they stop coming. When Master Patros looks up again, unshed tears make his eyes shiny. There's a new promise written in his gray eyes, but I can't fathom what it means. My heart's too full of the loss we're experiencing.

When Lady Gera's spirit leaves her body there's hardly a dry eye around us. Even Ryle looks disturbed by her death. Sara and young Etienne weep openly. They cling to each other like siblings losing a grandmother. Keeper Jemma summons servants to carry Lady Gera's body away. Killian stands off to the side looking anxious. Finally, he asks the question occupying every mind.

"What should we do?" Killian looks to his captain for an answer.

"Summon every guard," Captain Rillis instructs. "Have the squad commanders go through the tent camp below and ask for volunteers."

"I'll have my people prepare rooms for the refugees," offers Keeper Jemma. "We cannot leave them out there if an invading army is coming."

Keeper Jemma nearly crashes into Damien who looks paler than he did before, which is notable because the rest of his skin's a lovely light brown.

"A message for you, sir," says Damien. He hands the captain a thick arrow with green and white fletching.

Breaking the seal, Captain Rillis scans the note. He frowns and his eyes whip up to meet mine. The conflict and concern I read in his brown eyes says more than enough.

I stand and await his announcement.

"Give us the message, Rillis," says Huntmaster Beatrice.

Instead of saying it aloud, Rillis tosses the arrow to Beatrice. She reads the message and hands the bundle over to David Hart. He does the same and passes it on to Master Ori. The last to receive the scroll is Master Patros. When he understands, he shifts position to place his body between me and the rest of the council.

The servants stop moving, picking up on the sudden tension. Sara moves to my left side. She knows something's up even if she can't match words to it yet. Ryle takes a position to Sara's left and rests a hand on his dagger.

"What's going on?" asks Ryle.

"The message on the arrow comes from Supreme Huntmaster Jordan Lekros," explains Master Patros. "It explains the strength of the approaching forces and offers the temple peace in return for the girl."

Chapter 17:
Path to Caramore

The Lady
Central Meeting Chamber, Alamon Temple

I am tempted to switch my focus to Jordan Lekros's camp, but I need to see how the Keris Council chooses to handle his offer. That he made the offer at all is revealing. Much has changed within his heart. In Fort Amareth, Lekros was adamant that Oren cease using Bereft hostages to fulfill his contracts. What has the Outcast promised Lekros that makes him compromise his morals? Am I wrong about him? He could be deceived.

Master Patros's announcement of their situation has drawn the room into thirds. Keeper Jemma Heston is absent, having left to prepare the temple for the influx of refugees. Thanks to Lady Gera's last plea, Giovani Patros stands ready to defend my young Chosen Redeemer. Ryle and Sara stand with her. Victoria looks annoyed at being made a bargaining chip again. The fire of her spirit burns bright in the room, reminding me why I chose her to be my representative on Aeris.

Master Ori, Scribe Apprentice Etienne, and David Hart stand in the middle with most of the servants, unsure of what to do.

Captain Rillis and Huntmaster Beatrice occupy the space on the right side of the double doors to the chamber with most of the guards. Beatrice has her golden bow in hand but she's made no move to use it.

"We should consider the Supreme Huntmaster's proposal," Captain Rillis says reasonably. "We don't have enough soldiers to repel such a force."

"No, ye should not," Sara Andari retorts. "I come from

Coldhaven where we tried such a thing."

"Tried what?" asks David Hart.

"Turning Victoria over on command," Sara answers.

"And did it work?" presses Captain Rillis.

"Aye. It did for a short while," Sara admits. "But the peace didn't last. Denkari attacked that same night."

"It could be an unrelated incident," Huntmaster Beatrice observes.

"My point is that people who offer such bargains make the rules to suit their needs and change them at will," says Sara. "If ye sell Victoria, they may go away today, but ya can be sure they'll return when they want something else."

"We have nothing else they want," mutters Captain Rillis. "We're a collection of scholars, monks, and pilgrims who came to the mountains for fresh air."

"One army marching on the temple comes from the Darklands," Victoria reminds everybody. "We don't fit in the Outcast's plan for a new world. He hates us because we reflect the One too well. If we do not unite, the Outcast will pick us off one by one."

"She raises a good point," says Master Ori, the Keeper of Knowledge. "I say we help her."

"And I say we have a larger responsibility to the inhabitants of this sacred temple." Captain Rillis places his right hand on his sword. "Even if we fail at least we'll know we did everything in our power to prevent destruction."

Master Patros shapeshifts into a miniature red dragon. Even though he keeps the scale purposefully small, he fills the doorway, forcing the guards to back away to avoid being crushed. Captain Rillis shouts commands to his soldiers but I focus on Patros and Victoria.

"Come, child, climb aboard." Master Patros's voice sounds deeper and more authoritative in dragon form.

"I won't fight them," says Victoria, shaking her head sadly.

Giovani makes a low, rough laughing noise.

"I did not ask you to fight them," he says. "I think it best we leave with haste."

Victoria and Sara scramble up onto Master Patros's back, but Ryle refuses to join them.

"I must stay with my people," he explains, forcing a smile. "If you can summon aid, don't forget us."

Master Patros hisses when one of Huntmaster Beatrice's arrows finds the fleshy part of his back right foot. After carefully turning around in the doorway, he lumbers away from the Central Meeting Chamber. The floor shakes with each footfall. Despite being spacious under normal circumstances, the temple's hallways prevent Master Patros from flying. When they're three hallways away, he takes on his human form to lead them through narrow passages. They follow without hesitation. If Master Patros wanted to lead them into a trap, he could accomplish it easily.

Pushing the concern aside, I flood Victoria with the knowledge I think she'll need soon.

They meet the first real resistance when they reach the portal room. Captain Rillis must have had a Minder warn the guards to expect them. A line of five guards blocks their path.

Master Patros prepares to shift into a different combat form, but Victoria slips in front of him and approaches the guards.

"I seek passage into Caramore," she states.

"Nobody is allowed in by order of Captain Rillis," answers the middle guard. This one wears a fancier helmet than the others, marking him as a squad commander.

"Armies approach from three sides," Victoria informs the man. "You'll need to request help then destroy the portals soon." She knows the protocol because I told her about it.

Portal Guardians may wear temple guard uniforms, but they do not work for the temple. They answer to the Tariku League. It's not a widely known policy. Even the other guards look to their leader for confirmation of Victoria's statement.

"How do you know that?" asks the squad leader.

"My name is Victoria Saveron. The Lady, servant of Kailon, has told me so. I need to present myself to your leaders."

"Only Saroth have the right to speak to the council," says the man.

"My mother was Saroth," Victoria answers. "That means I at least have the right to present my case through a sponsor."

"Do you have a sponsor?" inquires the man.

"I will have one when I need it," Victoria replies. She tries not to think about where Katrina is right now.

I can do little more than assure the child that her friends still live.

"What should we do, Master Patros?" asks the head guard.

"Let her through," Master Patros replies.

"What about the other woman?" the guard presses. "She's no

Saroth."

Victoria casts an uncertain look at Sara. She is torn between urging her friend to stay behind and pleading with her to step into the unknown. I withdraw my presence from Victoria to avoid influencing her decision. The choice lies with Sara but she will place high emphasis on Victoria's wishes.

"What do you want to do, Sara?" Victoria asks.

"Make a decision quickly, my dear," urges Master Patros.

Heavy footsteps approach. Captain Rillis leads twenty guards in an effort to capture Victoria. If she doesn't leave soon, there will be a battle.

"I want to follow in yer footsteps wherever they may lead," says Sara.

With the decision made, Master Patros nods and gestures. The line of guards parts obediently, reforming once the three have stepped through. The head guard steps out of line and follows them while his men fill in the gap.

"Will you come too?" asks Victoria.

"No. This temple is my home," says Master Patros. "I will fight to preserve it."

"Thank ye for the aid, Master Patros." Sara follows the statement with a polite bow. "May the Lady save ye along with every soul here."

"We will return soon," Victoria promises. "Hopefully with the armies of Caramore behind us."

"Step through quickly," Master Patros instructs, waving to the two white portals hanging along the far wall. Gold letters atop the frame declare: Bastion and Dominance. "And don't look back. I am going to have Andros seal the portal behind you, so that none can follow along this path."

An arrow flies into the room over the heads of the guards and strikes the portal to Dominance. Knowing the attack may cause those on the receiving end to shut down the portal, Victoria and Sara sprint through.

In their haste, they stumble when the portal spits them out on the far side. The portal guards look highly agitated. One lies on the ground with an arrow in his left leg. Another guard tends to the wound. The rest form a tight circle around Victoria and Sara.

"Don't move." The speaker rests his sword on Victoria's left shoulder to emphasize the words. "Who are you? And what brings you to Caramore?"

Calmly, Victoria makes the introductions, outlines the situation at the Alamon Temple, and presents her request.

Once he understands who she is, the portal commander summons a Minder to seek instructions from his superiors. The wait lasts ten minutes during which time he allows them to stand. Finally, he receives orders to arrest Victoria and Sara and bring them before the council. The arrest order is extreme though not unheard of. Both young women submit to simple wrist bindings without protest. They're comforted by news that they're going where they wish to and the fact that they're together.

A pair of Destroyers escorts them up to the right chamber. They reach the waiting room before the council room and are met by an imposing older woman. At the woman's command, guards step out of the deeper shadows and remove Victoria's wrist bindings. Instead of releasing Sara, they take her by the elbows and lead her off to the side, leaving Victoria alone in the center of the dimly lit room.

The woman gracefully raises a hand, and the tiny orbs of light around the room brighten, allowing Victoria and Sara to see the lady clearly. She has graying black hair piled high on her head. Her black robes look expensive and she wears many necklaces, including a few brightly colored pendants. Sara gapes. Victoria looks from Sara to the woman and back again, confused by her friend's reaction. It's understandable, for Sara has the advantage of seeing the strong resemblance between them.

"Have you no greeting for your grandmother, Victoria?" inquires the woman.

Chapter 18:
Sponsor

Katrina Polani
Galeric's Camp, Plains of Forgiveness to Dominance
They struck Tellen nine times before Galeric was satisfied with the punishment. Had the first three blows landed across his back it would have been over, but the men always placed the third blow at the back of his knees. With the additional weight of the heavy beam across his shoulders, Tellen didn't have a chance of standing through the beating. By the end, he couldn't really stand at all. They leaned him up against the platform holding me. He'd lost consciousness after the sixth strike, which was merciful. A Healer made certain he would live, but wanted nothing to do with cleaning him up.

I volunteered, which is how we came to be locked in this cage together. Galeric thought it a fitting role for me. He can think what he likes. From the looks and smell of it, this cage probably housed the dog I set free tonight. I don't care. I'm simply grateful for the ability to help Tellen. The guilt's still heavy across my heart. One of the slave women brings me water warmed over a fire and clean rags to help with the cleaning. She cannot speak to me. Galeric has forbidden it, but I see the pity in her eyes.

The wounds across Tellen's back have begun to heal. While this is a wonderful discovery, I need to wake him up and hope he can consciously control the healing process. If Galeric discovers it, he'll find many reasons to hurt him. Galeric could order his Healer to formally tend the wounds, but the man's here by choice and would likely refuse such an order if he thought it futile.

"Tellen. Please wake up," I whisper, trying to keep the conversation private. I cover his back with the bloody rags to disguise the healing that's happening. "Galeric cannot know you can heal yourself."

I must have fallen asleep beside Tellen for the next thing I'm aware of is the thud of a body slumping to the ground outside the cage. The camp is quiet, and the fire has burned to embers. Two more thuds bring me fully awake. The lock on the gate sparks and falls away. A hand pulls the bars open.

"Katrina, come out of there," Adam calls softly.

"Adam?" I ask, not really believing my ears.

"Yes," he confirms. "Hurry, we must leave before the men awaken."

"I can't. Tellen's injured."

"All right. We'll come to you," Adam says to me. "In we go, little one."

I don't know who he's speaking to until a boy crawls into the cage with us. My twin brother takes his wolf form and crowds in behind the boy, squeezing past him to lie down next to Tellen.

"Take my hand and hold on to the man," says the boy solemnly. He holds his left hand out to me and places his right hand on Adam's back. "This might feel strange. Try not to move."

I've never seen a Specter before, and I don't get a decent look at this one until we arrive in the East Portal Room of the main building housing the Academy of Arts and Sciences. The boy is slightly younger than Vic, and he has sandy brown hair, brown eyes, and an easy smile. With a quick wave, the boy scampers off to the corner where a variety of toys and magic puzzles are stored.

Several people rush forward to help me up, but I ignore them in favor of checking on Tellen again. He's alive and no worse for wear than when we started, but he's still unconscious.

"Welcome home." A warm, familiar voice breaks through the noise.

My head whips toward my father.

The two portal guards and three attendants stop moving toward me. They part, creating a clear path for me to see my father. He's dressed in his usual dark blue ensemble. The sight of him draws me to my feet. I want to rush to him, but there's so much to say that I can't fathom where to begin. He closes the distance and embraces me briefly since there are witnesses. He's always been like that. I'm not surprised, but I'm a little disappointed. This is the first I've seen him in weeks since I was off on a training exercise with Master Talini before receiving my father's instructions to keep an eye on Vic.

Pulling me out to arm's length, my father systematically studies my face and body for signs of injury. I patiently wait out the ritual, taking comfort in the familiar behavior. The worry lines around his face are more distinct than I remember. I'm sure the same can be said for me. Much has changed since I last stood in my father's presence.

"We will talk after you've had a chance to refresh yourself and rest a bit," says my father. He waves to one of his people who promptly hands him a small metal device. With great care, Father traces the collar cinched around my neck with the metal rod, deactivating the gems. When the power has been drained, he draws a dagger and cuts the evil thing off of me.

I would fear for my life if the blade were wielded by anybody other than my father.

"What about Tellen?" I ask once I am free. I have to push past the urge to shapeshift just to feel the freedom of the different forms. "What will happen to him? He needs a Healer."

The portal guards have their hands on their weapons, and their attention rests on my friend.

My gaze lingers on Tellen for a long moment. The promise of rest is alluring, but I know that Tellen's likely to be treated like a prisoner rather than a guest if he's out of my sight.

"I will see to his needs," Adam offers.

For the first time, I look from Adam to my father and see how closely their features match. It's one matter to know a thing and another to see it confirmed. I trust Adam's word, but I'm still not convinced until my father speaks.

"You'll be allowed to see him later."

I'm not sure I like his wording, but the assurance is enough for now. Reluctantly, I follow one of the female attendants through the long corridors I know very well. This place is as much my home as my father's house outside of Jorash. My mother's murder when I was barely old enough to walk gave Father serious trust issues. He often brought me to work and had attendants and students watch over me.

This building takes up two city blocks, and most of the corridors are free for anybody to wander. My childhood self took full advantage of that freedom, especially after I accidentally discovered my ability to Shapeshift into a beetle. Master Talini has helped me refine and control the form, but I actually knew that one long before she showed it to me. That's something I'll not be telling Father or my master anytime soon. They don't know I've seen the prison in the lower levels or peered into the lofty chambers where the various councils meet. I try not to think about the prison because I'm still not certain what Tellen's fate will be. Justified or not, my people don't trust Arkonai.

Eventually, we reach the wing that houses the female students, faculty, and guest rooms. To my surprise, my old room has been prepared for me. My father hardly ever kept regular hours. Sleepovers at the Academy were a regular occurrence during my childhood.

One of my fancier dresses has been laid across the small bed. It's a seafoam green color with a simple design from the waist down. The waist itself is marked by a long silk belt cinched at the front with a gold buckle. From the waist up, the dress features several folds that give the middle character. The bust has pleats. Light green lace studded with tiny gemstones outlines the bust in a manner that makes it look like miniature vines. The most striking part about the dress is the sheer green cape that accompanies it. There's a piece that drapes around one's neck and clasps at the front then flows down left and right until it wraps around one's arms, leaving the shoulders bare.

I wonder what Tellen will think of the dress. He's never actually seen me wear one before. The thought makes me nervous. I should dig around in the closet until I find something more practical for fighting in, but for now, I'll wear what's been set out for me.

The dress tells me the debriefing to come may be more formal than expected. The attendant points out the steaming hot bath prepared for me and asks if I need anything. I thank her and send her away. Once alone, I remove the filthy clothes I've worn for weeks. While traveling with the people of Sorrow Falls we had a few chances to wash our clothes in small streams. However, Galeric's men were far less keen on such niceties.

Although I'd like nothing better than to sit in the tub for hours, I scrub myself quickly. I'll need to answer many questions before asking any, and I'm eager to know if Vic made it to Caramore yet. Getting into the dress is a little complicated without help, but I manage with some creative shapeshifting. I turn into a beetle, crawl inside, and transform back into human form. I hesitate before donning the cape and its collar. Bad memories of the last collar I wore assail me.

When I report to the attendant standing outside my room, she leads me to my father's office. He's seated behind the large wooden desk with its intricate carvings on the sides. I remember adding my own carving on the rare occasions he left me alone in his office. Upon seeing me, my father rises. Adam stands off to the side studying a map that takes up much of the wall to my right.

"Your report will have to be made on the way to the High Council's antechamber," says my father.

I furrow my brows to convey my confusion.

"Vic needs a sponsor," Adam explains.

"She's here?" My voice sails high with disbelief and my mind races to comprehend Adam's statement. I know we were delayed, but I'm not sure how Vic got through the portal from the Alamon Temple.

"Is she the Chosen Redeemer?" My father steps up next to me and grips my left arm.

"I believe so," I answer.

"Then we must help her," says Father. Releasing my arm, he strides quickly to the door with Adam a half-step behind.

I have to jog to keep up. This requires concentration since the cloth slippers that go with the dress aren't made for walking or running. I suddenly miss the sturdy boots I'd worn throughout the recent adventures.

"What's wrong?" I call after my father.

"I'm not sure anything is wrong," replies my father, "but I am loath to leave the girl alone with Lady Corabelle for long."

Corabelle Castaloni is the mother of Vic's late mother, Marina. She's also one of the most powerful members of the Tariku League and has been for several years. By extension, that means she's manipulative, cunning, and dangerous. If she chooses to support Vic, she would be a powerful ally, but given the stance Vic's uncle has taken, I'm not very hopeful of that outcome. Everybody knows that Jackson Castaloni has always been his mother's favorite child.

I'd always assumed I would be Vic's sponsor when she presented the situation to the council, but if Lady Corabelle knows Vic's here, the odds are good Jackson will have the same knowledge soon. I do not like that prospect. He's shown far too much interest in Vic and her magic bracers. I draw comfort from the idea that Jackson will likely not threaten Vic within the Academy walls, but I wouldn't put it past him to cause trouble any way he can.

My fears prove well-founded when our small party enters the High Council's waiting room. Vic stands in the center looking like a bug caught in a spider's web. Lady Corabelle and Jackson Castaloni stand across from her near the doors leading to the inner chamber.

Swallowing an uneasy lump in my throat, I glide to Vic's side so that she sees me before moving around behind her and putting my hands on her shoulders.

"I will sponsor Victoria Saveron," I declare. "She will be my guest and I will be her guardian." This is what needs to happen since Vic's only half-Saroth. Otherwise, she won't be recognized as a citizen and granted the right to address the council.

"What a wonderful idea," says Jackson with a creepy smile. "I will make the same offer."

My heart sinks like a stone kicked off a cliff.

"I acknowledge the offer of sponsorship from both parties," says Lady Corabelle. "As I can only grant one request, I must honor the fact that Jackson's claim is stronger."

Although I made the offer first, Jackson is kin to Vic. Bloodlines mean everything.

My young friend stiffens and steps back into my arms. She's trembling, and I think she has good reason to do so.

Chapter 19:
Cleansed and Clothed

Victoria Saveron
Academy of Arts and Sciences, City of Dominance
I don't understand what just happened, but Katrina's voice sounds strained when she addresses my grandmother and my uncle.

"Please allow me to prepare her for the audience with the High Council."

"Thank you, but that won't be necessary," says Grandmother. She speaks in the same crafty way that tells me where Uncle Jack picked up his penchant for scheming. "I've summoned servants to see to that task. They'll be here shortly."

My stomach twists at her words. She put in the request a moment ago, giving the order to the same Destroyers who escorted Sara and me through the city. The pair left to carry out Grandmother's orders, taking Sara with them.

"I would like to stay with Katrina." I make a conscious effort to stop shaking, but the room has felt incredibly chilly since Uncle Jack magically appeared here a few minutes ago.

"She has other matters to attend to." Grandmother's dismissive tone is reinforced by a casual wave.

Katrina's arms tighten around my waist instinctively. Soft silk from her cape surrounds me. The beadwork and decorative lace make my head itch, but I don't dare move.

"Like what?" Katrina demands.

Uncle Jack's half-smile convinces me I won't like Grandmother's answer.

"Like seeing to the well-being of the young Arkonai rescued at the same time she was." On the surface, my grandmother's words sound like they contain genuine concern, but I hear the sharp threat hidden beneath. "Without an advocate to plead his innocence, he could be treated as a spy."

Tellen, like Sara, is now a hostage.

"Vic?" Katrina whispers in my ear. Her inflection turns my name into a question. She wants to know what I think she should do.

Spinning in her arms, I catch hold of Katrina's hands and squeeze them tightly. She's wearing a beautiful sea green dress that complements her eye color well.

"Help him," I say. Releasing her hands, I take a small step backward. "Check on Sara too. I'm not sure what's become of her."

"I don't believe we'll need to hear testimony from the Bereft girl. Thus, she is resting from her long travels," Grandmother assures us. "Would you like her at the hearing?"

"If she wants to be there," I say cautiously.

Grandmother's rich, light laughter fills the room.

"What a safe answer, Victoria," she comments. "You'll have to be bolder when you appear before the Tariku League."

The same two Destroyers reenter the room and nod solemnly to Grandmother.

Uncle Jack waves them forward impatiently.

"Clean up the child and have her back here quick as you can," he instructs the pair.

They bristle but make no move to do anything until Grandmother inclines her head briefly.

"The Council will be assembled soon," Grandmother says, "but see that she's clean, given something to eat, and properly attired before returning her here."

The Destroyers exchange nervous glances.

"There should be something suitable in my quarters," Katrina offers. Her words sound cold and aloof. "I'm certain you can find the way there without me. I am needed elsewhere." Softening her tone, Katrina directs her last words to me. "I will try to make it to the hearing."

This day has not gone to plan. I follow the Destroyers through long corridors to a section with doors lining both sides. For their part, the Destroyers say little and look like they're ready for an ambush at any second. Torches light most halls, though there are a few that contain hovering orbs of light or glowing balls of blue-white energy confined within glass cases mounted on the walls. I've never seen any place like this. The building is enormous.

The Destroyers turn me over to a pair of ordinary servants at the door to Katrina's quarters. I didn't even know she had a room here. She never mentioned it, but I suppose there wasn't a great opportunity for that to come up in conversation between running from the zombies and trying not to get killed by my uncle.

Once tucked inside the room, the women efficiently strip off my clothes and toss me into a warm bath. They try to remove the silver bracelets, but I gently let them know that's not possible.

For a second, I think they're out to drown me. One holds my head under water before lifting me up and dumping a sweet smelling liquid into my hair. I hadn't given my hair much thought until the woman runs a strange contraption over it, causing considerable pain as each hair protests being moved. My expression must convey my fright because the woman calmly explains that it's a brush for keeping hair nice. Father always made sure I kept a decent comb and cut my hair before the need for more arose. Eventually, the tangles yield to the brush, and the experience almost becomes pleasant.

I wonder how they knew Katrina would offer the use of her room, but given the amount of Minders wandering these halls, I guess I shouldn't be surprised by anything.

After drying me off, the servants direct me to don white linen underclothes and a white slip before pulling a dark dress over my head. I've seen many village women wear dresses, though none quite this fine. It's a simple dress compared to the one Katrina currently wears, but the fabric's soft and supple. Most of the dress is a plain color somewhere between blue and black, but the sleeves and the collar are outlined by a multi-colored strip of cloth. Likewise, a belt about three finger-widths apart of the same fabric encircles my waist before flowing down the front of the dress toward the ground. It feels too big until the women tighten the red ties woven up and down both sides. Once secured in the dress, I move to put on my old cloth boots, but one of the servants stops me.

"Sit on the bed there," she instructs. "I have just the thing to complete this."

I do so.

With unexpected ceremony, the woman kneels before me and slips a pair of sandals onto my feet.

Thanking the women, I rise to leave, but once again, they redirect me. This time, I'm shown over to a small table with a single chair where a tray of food awaits. The fare consists of a cold piece of meat, a warm slice of bread, and several kinds of fruit. A glass containing a deep red liquid sits next to the large plate, but I ignore it in favor of pouring myself a cup of water from the carafe sitting against the wall. My stomach rumbles at the sight of the food. It's been many hours since the morning meal.

"Drink the water, but do not consume the food. One will give strength. The other will require it."

The voice that fills me belongs to the One. I'm so startled at hearing it that I drop the fork I'd picked up to try the meat.

"What's the matter, child?" asks the woman who had washed and brushed my hair.

"I'm not hungry." Another rumble from my stomach declares the statement a lie.

"Please eat," pleads the other woman. She wrings her hands. Her accent tells me she's probably from one of the southwestern Bereft villages. I wonder what brought her to Caramore. Is she a captive? Is she a pilgrim? "The blame will fall to us if ye appear weak before the council."

"I won't," I promise. Picking up the cup of water, I drain it. I mean to only take a sip, but when the cool, sweet water touches my tongue, I have to finish it. "The One, whom I serve, will uphold me."

The last statement comes from me, but I recognize that the words are not truly my own. I am merely echoing them. The second woman and I enter into a short staring contest, but eventually, she nods.

"Your eyes do appear brighter," notes the first woman. "That will have to do for now."

"May I know your names?" I ask.

They are Hannah Meris and Aaliyah Naphtel. The next few minutes pass swiftly while they share their stories with me. Though they are not slaves, they serve in the Academy to keep loved ones out of prison. Apparently, in Caramore, one can willingly pay another's debt if both parties and the government reach an agreement. Hannah's son and Aaliyah's brother were convicted of smuggling dragon eggs. Their sentences would have stretched the span of three lifetimes had the women not stepped up and assumed part of the punishment. The judge commuted their sentences to seven years of labor if the women served in the Academy for the same time.

By the end of our time together, they feel like friends. I encourage them to drink the water but tell them not to eat any of the fine food on the tray. When the two Destroyers return for me, both women give me fierce hugs. I'm usually not much for sentiment, but I find myself fighting tears.

My heart dwells with the servants throughout the trip back to the chamber where I first met my grandmother. After sweeping her gaze up and down my body, Grandmother inclines her head, whirls, and pushes aside the heavy double doors separating this room from the council's meeting chamber.

Uncle Jack steps out of the shadows and moves to my side. He offers me his elbow and I tentatively take it and let him escort me into the room.

The room's much bigger than I imagined it would be, and it's set up like a court sketch I saw in a book once. Nine large, throne-like chairs line the far wall on a raised platform in a semi-circle shape. The middle chair rises a few feet higher than the others. A curved table springs out to the right and left of the center podium, which is well above them. A simple metal bar rises up out of the floor in front of the council members. It doesn't take much imagination to picture a prisoner being chained there to await his or her fate.

My grandmother slowly ascends the stairs on the right side of the platform and takes a seat to the left of the main podium.

As we reach the bar, Uncle Jack stops and leans over to whisper instructions.

"Have a care with your words in here, and let me do the talking."

"You have to let them know that the Alamon Temple is about to be overrun," I tell Uncle Jack. I try not to think about the very real possibility that the pending attack might have been orchestrated by my uncle. "They have to help!"

"They don't have to do anything," Uncle Jack reminds me.

"Present your case, Jackson Castaloni," orders the large man sitting at the center of the council. His wild white hair swings from side to side. He gestures for Uncle Jack to get on with it. "Why have you called for this meeting?"

The question alarms me. I want to shout that it's not him, it's me calling for the meeting, but nothing comes out when I open my mouth to speak.

"Ah, it appears Mother has taken measures to ensure good behavior," comments Uncle Jack. He nods behind me.

I turn and see Sara, Katrina, and Tellen occupying one of the benches. A line of guards stands behind them. Katrina's expression is hard to read. Tellen looks pale and angry. Sara looks serene. Noticing my attention, she gives me an encouraging smile. One of the men standing behind the bench doesn't fit with the others. He doesn't look happy with what he sees. It takes me a long second to realize why. He must be Katrina's father. There's something in the way he holds himself and inclines his head that reinforces the idea.

"Who is this fair-haired child standing before us?" the man continues, pulling my attention back to the front.

"My humblest apologies, Speaker," offers Uncle Jack, bowing deeply to the man. "The girl before you is my niece, Victoria Saveron, daughter of my late sister, Marina." He stops to let the council members take in that information. He folds a hand over his heart and looks at me with a strange mixture of pity and malice. "So, you will understand that it is with a heavy heart that I come before you to say that she's delusional. She goes around claiming to be the Chosen Redeemer, and furthermore, she's responsible for opening Darkland portals."

Chapter 20:
The Trial

The Lady
Main Council Chambers of the Tariku League, City of Dominance
Shock rolls through the room. The soldiers guarding Victoria's friends physically restrain them to keep them in their seats. Speaker Marco Neri bangs his gavel to restore order. Victoria gapes at her uncle, feeling betrayed.

"That is a very serious accusation," says Speaker Neri. "What is your proof?"

"I am a witness," Jackson declares. He waves to Victoria's friends. "As are these young people. They may deny it in an effort to protect my misguided niece, but you can compel them to speak truth if you cast the right spell."

One by one, Victoria's friends are called forth to bear witness. A Minder casts a simple truth spell over them and poses carefully worded questions which they're only allowed to answer with a "yes" or a "no."

"Did the accused open a Darkland portal in your presence?" the Minder asks Sara Andari.

"Yes," she answers. When she tries to say more, she loses her voice. Frustrated tears spring to her eyes as she fights the spell.

"Has she claimed to be the Chosen Redeemer?" presses the Minder.

"No." Sara struggles to say more, but her throat closes over the words, making her cough instead.

Jackson exchanges a long look with his mother.

"I think this once, it may help to hear the girl's explanation," says

Lady Corabelle to the Speaker.

Nodding thoughtfully, the Speaker waves for the Minder to lift the spell for a moment.

"You may elaborate," says the Minder.

"Victoria has made no such claim of being the Chosen Redeemer, but I can see that she is what others claim." Sara falls silent as the Minder reasserts the spell.

Tellen and Katrina endure similar interrogations, though his is much shorter because the Saroth do not trust his word.

"Lady Corabelle, do you have anything you wish to add before we cast our votes on this matter?" inquires Speaker Neri.

Corabelle Castaloni looks down from her high chair upon Victoria. By this time, the girl leans heavily upon the bar meant to confine prisoners. Seizing upon the smallest spark of pity, I silently plead with the woman to come to her granddaughter's defense.

"Let her speak," says Corabelle.

Jackson shoots his mother an alarmed look.

"She'll speak lies," Jackson protests.

"She cannot speak lies within these walls," Speaker Neri reminds Jackson. He gestures to the Minder controlling the simple truth spell, and the woman makes a subtle adjustment to the spell. Facing Victoria, the Speaker studies the blond child. "All right, girl, you've heard the accusations. What have you to say about them?"

I channel a spirit of calmness and confidence into Victoria. Her spirit reaches out for the right words to say.

"I came here to beg your aid. You know what approaches the Alamon Temple. Your Minders have seen it. Without your army, they will perish."

"That temple is well beyond our borders," notes the councilman sitting to the far left if one sees the members from Victoria's point of view. "Those who dwell there know the risks."

"But what seeks to destroy the temple is only a symptom of a larger problem," Victoria says.

I flood the girl with every scrap of information I've gathered.

"What sort of problem?" asks the Speaker. He folds his hands on the table and favors Victoria with a patronizing smile.

"War," Victoria replies. "Somebody or something wants a war that will steal our hope and dash our dreams before claiming our lives."

"If you want to prevent this war you speak of, why did you open Darkland portals?" The Speaker's tone makes the question an accusation.

I caution Victoria not to bring the focus to Jackson Castaloni.

"I was compelled to do so," she answers.

"I think we've heard enough from the delusional child," says Jackson, ignoring Victoria. "But before you cast your votes, allow me to present my proposal."

"And pray tell, what is that?" Speaker Neri's tone grows impatient.

"Grant me custody of her," Jackson requests. "Allow me to raise her. I believe I can steer her in the right direction. Too much time in the woods has led to these flights of fancy. Her mother was my sister after all. It's the least I can do to honor her memory."

The noise level in the room rises. Victoria looks hard at her uncle, trying to understand his motivations. There must be enough truth to his statement, but I am not convinced he has her best interests in his heart.

"What say you to your uncle's proposal, girl?" asks Speaker Neri.

"I have a father," replies Victoria.

"That may be," says the Speaker. "But if you're to remain here, you must have a Saroth sponsor. That is the role your uncle is currently fulfilling."

"I don't intend to stay here, sir," Victoria assures the Speaker. She glances at each of the other council members in turn. "I must travel to my father's people and give them the same message. Both sides must guard their hearts and minds against misgivings that are centuries old. The Outcast and his servants are the only enemies we ought to have."

"You want us to join the Arkonai?" The Speaker's question contains enough disdain to convey his derision. "They're going around slaughtering our people!" His dark eyes blaze with anger, and he glares over Victoria's shoulder at young Tellen.

The three on the bench surrounded by guards look ready to burst with the need to speak.

"Let my friends speak from their hearts," Victoria says. "Our only goal is to save lives, and the best means to accomplish that is to unite the Arkonai and the Saroth."

After a short debate, the council members decide to let Tellen, Sara, and Katrina make short statements in exchange for answering any questions posed to them. Jackson fumes at Victoria's side.

Tellen steps forward first.

"What have you to say about the Resolute hunting Saroth?" asks the Speaker. "Do you deny they are Arkonai?"

"I deny nothing, but they do not represent the whole of my people," Tellen answers.

"How can you say that when your Supreme Huntmaster sides with them?" wonders Lady Corabelle.

"I cannot speak for him, madam," says Tellen, "but I was sent here by my father with the blessing of the High Council to pursue a path to peace."

The Tariku League members spend a few more minutes peppering Tellen with questions, but he fields them with ease. Next, their attention turns to Sara Andari.

"This is a rather strange party," notes Speaker Neri. "How did you come to travel with them?"

"A huntsman called Oren took me away from me home in Coldhaven to force Victoria to submit to his will," Sara answers. "Once the others arrived and broke us free, I chose to stay because I believe in what they stand for."

"Who hired this huntsman?" presses the Speaker.

Sara hesitates because she feels my warning upon her heart, but the truth spell still lingers in the air.

"Supreme Huntmaster Jordan Lekros and that man there, Jackson Castaloni."

Her announcement causes chaos. The nine council members come to their feet. The guards move forward to protect the Bereft girl, but Jackson's far closer. Drawing a dagger from within the folds of his cloak, Jackson draws Sara into a tight embrace and holds the blade at her throat.

"Jackson!" cries Lady Corabelle. "What is the meaning of this?"

The air crackles with energy. The Destroyers prepare to fill the room with lightning.

"My apologies, Mother," says Jackson. "I tried to do this the simple way, but I cannot wait for the Council to favor me in these matters. I'm taking Victoria. Send for a Specter." His ability to Conjure himself from place to place does not stretch to another let alone to two young ladies.

"We will not negotiate with you," the Speaker announces coldly. "If you serve the Outcast, you'll do so alone."

The silence that falls after the Speaker's declaration is complete.

A strong peace still rests on Victoria, but I feel her reaching out for advice. I make it clear that the choice is fully hers. Sara will likely die if Victoria does not go with her uncle. Jackson is filled with dark energy that will stunt the small influence I wield on this world. An idea occurs to me. Perhaps I can lend some aid. I set those plans in motion and tell Victoria to stall.

"I will." Victoria's statement is soft but loud in the silent room.

"You'll what?" Jackson's tension causes him to increase the pressure on Sara's neck.

"I'll negotiate with you," Victoria clarifies.

"Do you want to die, girl?" asks the Speaker. "Besides, what can you do?"

Victoria regards the Speaker and the Council carefully before answering.

"I can open a portal."

One may wonder why I kept that knowledge from Victoria before now, and the answer is simple. Only a being filled with extremes of light or dark or perfect neutrality can survive the portal she intends to create, for it requires the traveler to step into and out of the Darklands. With my grace resting upon her, Victoria can weather the journey, but I previously felt she needed to stay with her companions.

"To where?" inquires Jackson.

"To the Darklands," intones the Speaker. His Minder capabilities have allowed him to pick up on Victoria's plan.

"I will seal it once we're through," Victoria promises, nodding to confirm the Speaker's intuition. Turning to her uncle, she continues, "But you'll have to let Sara go. Only you and I can safely step into and out of that place."

"What guarantee would I have of your compliance?" Jackson wonders.

"Me," says Katrina.

"Absolutely not," declares Marcus Polani.

"Transformation magic is inherently neutral. Any animal form should be able to travel in the Darklands," Katrina explains for the benefit of Tellen and Sara.

Victoria looks stricken, but I confirm that her friend speaks truth.

Jackson's smile contains triumph.

"Excellent." Snapping the fingers of his left hand, Jackson conjures another collar like the one he gave to Galeric to control Katrina.

Most of the onlookers draw sharp breaths when they spot the evil artifact.

He tosses the collar to Victoria. It lands at her feet.

"Pick it up," Jackson instructs. "Have your friend assume her dog form and put that on her."

While usually meant to keep someone in their human form, such a collar can prevent shifts to any form.

"No! I forbid it!" shouts Marcus.

Two of his people restrain him.

Stooping, Victoria picks up the collar and turns to Katrina.

"Are you sure about this?"

"I'm going with you," Katrina declares. She eyes the evil thing in Victoria's hands. "If that's the price, so be it."

Without further ado, Katrina turns herself into a dog and pads over to Victoria, whining softly to lend comfort.

With tears blurring her vision and sobs locking her throat, Victoria throws her arms around Katrina's neck and hugs her. When she withdraws, she applies the device that will imprison her friend in dog form. Jackson beckons and Katrina trots over to him. He releases Sara and repositions the dagger. The threat moves to Katrina.

Unable to voice words, Victoria shifts to a kneeling position and prays the ancient phrases silently. Slowly, a portal materializes next to her. It hovers in the air, drawing every eye to itself. No matter which side one looks through, black, swirling mist fills the portal.

"After you," says Jackson with mock courtesy.

With one last look at her remaining friends, Victoria rises and steps through the portal.

Chapter 21:
Guardian Pact

Katrina Polani
Combat Arena, Fort Medron

Vic's portal leads us into the Darklands. I do not like this place, especially the smell. It feels evil, and there's a faint hint of death in the air. The colors here are muted like they forgot what they were and are only a shadow of their former selves. We're in a field, but the plants look ill. There's a sun in the sky, but it's hazy. There's a breeze, but it's warm and clingy instead of refreshing.

Jackson Castaloni has a firm grip upon the collar preventing me from shapeshifting. I have to restrain myself to keep from biting his hand. A low, defensive growl escapes me, warning nearby spirits that pause to regard us.

"Now, take us to Fort Medron," Jackson instructs Vic.

"I don't know where that is," says Vic. "It might take me a moment to find it."

With that, Vic stretches forth her hands and opens a new portal. The picture inside this portal shows a village surrounded by forests on three sides. The edges are slightly blurry, like one's looking through ice-encrusted glass. Instead of stepping through, Vic murmurs words in a beautiful language I don't recognize.

"Queldom paricce?"

"What are you saying?" Jackson's grip on the collar tightens, but I'm too busy concentrating on Vic and the new portal to care much.

"I'm asking the portal where it leads," Vic explains.

I don't hear anything, but Vic must get an answer from the portal because she makes a swiping gesture that causes the portal to shimmer, turn completely white, and settle on a new picture. This time the portal shows a tall, snow-capped mountain. Vic repeats her question and gestures again and again. The portal shifts several times until settling on an imposing stone structure.

"That's it," says Jackson.

"Alam," Vic commands the portal.

No translation's needed for the portal's image becomes crystal clear and it lowers to the ground in front of us. Vic steps through first followed quickly by me and Jackson. Once through, I'm relieved to encounter the normal collection of scents I can pick up in dog form. I smell a young child, but a quick look around does not reveal him. The scents associated with him are that of chicken grease, dirt, sweat, and parchment. The other dominating smells are mildew, blood, fear, and the cloying scent of dead things from beyond. Something dark entered the world in this place.

We've arrived in a sandy pit. While most of the sand is a blend of white or yellow, the particles in the center are pitch-black. Chains decorate the stone walls at even intervals.

Vic faces her uncle.

"Let me send Katrina back," Vic says.

I shake my head vigorously. For better or worse, I want to stay with her.

"Looks like she disagrees with you," Jackson comments.

"At least take the collar off," Vic pleads.

I look to Jackson for his answer though I'm not hopeful it'll be favorable.

"I kind of like her this way," says Jackson. He tugs on the collar and leads me to the left wall. There, he fixes one of the sturdy chains to the collar.

Sitting down to watch the proceedings, I ponder ways to break free.

Sighing, Vic lets the portal close and fade away.

"Why am I here?" Vic asks, directing the question to her uncle.

"You're here because I wish it so." The male voice that speaks has a pleasant, inviting quality to it, but Vic flinches at the sound.

Vic's magic bracers light up and morph into their long, defensive form which covers her forearms completely.

Our gazes lock on a dark figure that materializes a short distance from Vic. A faint spirit aura glows around the man before dissipating. Long, golden hair hangs well past his shoulders, held back by a thin, gold band. His features are rugged and handsome, but he carries a dark scent with him. The smell brings my hackles up, and I growl at him. His dark clothes reek of misery, death, and fire. Reaching out, the man moves to touch Vic's face, but stops with his hand hovering near her left cheek.

"Order her to take the bracers off," the man instructs Jackson. He withdraws his hand and glances down at the silver armor engulfing Vic's arms.

"I ... can't," Jackson admits, looking deeply uncomfortable. "We left before the Council granted me guardianship. The bracers still belong to her father."

The handsome man's face twists with rage and he glares at Jackson.

"Fool!" he rages. "You'll pay for this!"

With that declaration still ringing in our ears, the man disappears.

"What just happened?" Vic asks. Her bracers remain in their larger form, telling us something with powerfully dark magic is close. When she gets no answer from her uncle, Vic poses two more questions. "Where did the Dark Man go? Why would it matter if you were my guardian?"

I find the title fitting.

"If you were legally my ward, everything you own would become partially mine," Jackson explains. "In theory, that would let me take them from you."

I get the feeling he would normally ignore such a question, but he's trying not to dwell on the spirit man's last words.

"What's so important about them?" Vic wonders, staring down at the magical bracers. "I don't even think you could use them."

"Oh, it's not about him using them, Victoria," says the Dark Man, returning to the exact spot he'd vacated scant seconds before. "It's about depriving you of their protection."

"Why would you want to turn me into a mindless zombie?" Vic asks.

Her question draws a deep chuckle from the handsome man. The chuckle soon shifts into peals of laughter.

"Your ignorance is delightful." The Dark Man beams at my friend.

"Then enlighten me." Vic's tone hardens with irritation.

"In due time," the man promises with a careless wave. "We must await the arrival of a very special guest."

"What are you talking about?" asks Jackson.

"Uncle Jack?" calls a young boy. "What's going on?"

"Alec!" Jackson cries. The fear in his words makes me pay attention. "Get out of here!"

"Vic!" the dark-haired child cries. His whole body brightens as he clambers into the arena and races over to Vic.

Jackson tries to grab the boy but misses.

The child's embrace knocks Vic back a half-step. She returns the hug, but looks perplexed.

"Victoria Saveron, meet your cousin, Alec Castaloni," says the man with mock formality. "Your mother and his father were siblings of your dear Uncle Jack."

Alec turns around in Vic's arms and watches his uncle and the Dark Man carefully. Her arms still drape protectively over his shoulders.

I whine, sensing the Dark Man's evil intent. He disappears again and reappears halfway across the sandy arena. Reaching forward, he makes a quick grabbing gesture. Alec flies out of Vic's arms and lands on his knees in front of the Dark Man. With another, more elaborate wave the man conjures a wicked-looking dagger. Its silver surface shines in the bright light coming from Vic's bracers.

"Let him go." Vic's tone splits the line between a plea and a demand.

"I would love to," says the Dark Man, "but unfortunately, your uncle needs to be punished for his many failures."

"They're my failures." The tremor in Jackson's voice tells me he genuinely cares for Alec. "Don't harm the boy because of them."

"Silence!" orders the Dark Man.

Without warning, he mentally pushes Jackson away until his back meets the stone wall directly opposite of me. The chains move of their own accord, cinching tight across his wrists, ankles, and waist. Another chain wraps around his neck and draws his head up at an odd angle.

Despite the endless trouble his scheming has caused us, sorrow fills my heart when I gaze at Jackson.

The Dark Man strikes an exaggerated thinking pose.

Alec's body rises off the ground and hovers in the air to Vic's left. The boy hangs by his arms like a scarecrow. His head slumps to the side.

"That's better," comments the Dark Man. "Now we can talk in peace. Allow me to explain my problem."

I bark a warning to my friend, but I'm helpless to intervene. A broad bolt of lightning crashes into Vic, flinging her back toward the stone wall to my left. Her bracers brighten and stop her momentum before impact. She lands lightly on her feet. Smoke curls up from a hole in the center of the dark dress she wears, but there's not even a singed hair on her.

"*That* is my problem," continues the Dark Man. "You're under the Lady's grace, and I need you to willingly lay it down so I can kill you."

Something heavy and oppressive falls over my spirit, ending my furious barks. The feeling is a thousand times more potent than the draining touch of the Denkari. I sink to the ground barely able to hold my head up.

Vic's gaze moves from the Dark Man to me to Alec to her uncle and back to the Dark Man.

"Why do you want me dead?" Vic wonders. She looks and sounds far calmer than someone in her situation ought to.

"Focus on the consequences of not complying, my dear," suggests the Dark Man. "Your cousin will die. Even your friend will die. I'd kill your uncle too if I didn't think that would be a favor to you."

"I need to understand," Vic presses. "What does my death gain you?"

The Dark Man doesn't answer, but Vic's head tilts slightly to the side and she nods.

"Relief from that," says the Dark Man with a dramatic sigh. "As the Lady's Chosen Redeemer, you are probably the closest thing to a savior this pitiful world has. Your death will require her to spend much time and effort replacing you. I'm going to use that time to burn this land to oblivion."

Vic draws a breath and closes her eyes, probably to converse with the Lady.

"How will I know you'll spare them if I'm dead?" asks Vic.

The question means she's considering the proposal.

"You'll have to trust me." The Dark Man smiles warmly. "I've nothing special to be gained by ending the boy, and your friend can safely wait out the war in one of my dungeons."

I whine. She shouldn't trust the Dark Man. He's incapable of truth.

"Swear an oath that you will not harm them," says Vic.

Anger washes over the Dark Man's features. Alec's body floats closer to him, and he touches the dagger to the boy's throat.

"The only promise you'll get is his death if you don't obey right now."

"All right!" Vic whispers. She drops to her knees and folds her hands together. Soon, her bracers shrink back to their bracelet form. Slowly, Vic eases the left bracer off with her right hand. Next, she eases the right bracer off and lets the pair tumble from her fingers.

My mournful howl rivals the Dark Man's triumphant shout. He mentally pulls Vic forward. I watch in slow motion as her body meets the blade in his outstretched hand. He eases her down to her knees, still holding tight to the dagger he buried in her stomach.

Flashes of light nearly blind everybody and two figures appear.

The Dark Man's victory cry turns to one of rage.

As my dazzled eyes adjust, I recognize Tellen and Shadow. Both clutch their sides, but in another second, they stand straighter and draw their weapons, standing guard over Vic.

Chapter 22:
Return to the Temple

Victoria Saveron
Combat Arena, Fort Medron

The Lady's promise that I would not die today surrounds my heart with warmth and light, but does little for the pain coursing throughout my body with every heartbeat. I'm dimly aware that Tellen and Shadow have arrived to my left and right respectively. Breaking into a cold sweat, I roll onto my back in time to see Shadow mentally beckon my bracers. They slip into place on my wrists and relief floods me. There's still pain, but it shrinks to a level where I can think again.

Shrieking, the Outcast fires several bolts of lightning at us. Tellen ducks the one aimed at him. Shadow forms a shield that redirects a few bolts into the sand at our feet, and I catch two with my bracers. They impact harmlessly. Frustrated, the Outcast adjusts his aim to kill Alec.

I'm in front of the boy before the lightning bolt is fully formed.

The Outcast holds it like a staff. It casts an eerie glow on his face.

"We've seen through your lies," I declare. "And we will tell everybody about them. Your reign of terror will come to an end very soon."

"Your power weakens every moment of every day," Tellen adds.

"Be gone," says Shadow.

"I sense I'm not welcome here," says the Outcast. "We will finish this another day, Chosen Redeemer. Next time, I think I'll make you come to me."

The Outcast's last statement worries me, but I try to bury the feeling.

Ripping a hole in the Veil, the Outcast steps through. He stands on the threshold of the portal he's created, reaches back through into this world, and gestures toward Uncle Jack. The chains holding my uncle to the wall break. He flies into the portal. It slams shut as soon as he's through.

Suddenly lightheaded, I sway and start to fall over.

"That can't be good," Shadow notes. He reaches out, catches me, and eases me to the ground.

I'm not sure if he's referring to Uncle Jack disappearing into the Veil with the Outcast or my weak knees.

Tellen's over by Katrina removing the terrible collar. Once back in human form, she tackles him with a tight embrace. She's still wearing the pretty green dress. There's something different about them, but my brain's too numb to pick at that right now.

In the stillness that follows, we hear muffled sobs. Twisting my head to the right, I see Alec huddled on the sand. He has his arms wrapped around his knees and his head resting on his arms.

"Help me up," I say to Shadow.

He's still hovering nearby.

"Lie down," he says, ignoring my request. "I need to check that wound."

"We need to help him," I protest, waving to Alec.

"He's fine," Shadow argues. "You're the one who got stabbed."

"How do you know that?" I ask. "You weren't even here for that part."

"What do you think brought us here?" Shadow points to a spot on the left side of his stomach, exactly where I'd felt the dagger bite me. "I was in Cardeth when I felt the pull."

"And I was in Dominance," says Tellen. "We were brought here by our contract with you."

He's walking back hand-in-hand with Katrina.

Tugging free of his grip, Katrina goes to Alec, sits next to him, and pulls him into a hug. The comfort increases the sobs for a while.

Taking advantage of my distraction, Shadow knocks me to a prone position. Borrowing one of Tellen's daggers, he carefully cuts part of the dress away and inspects the wound. I strain to see. A long, angry red line shows the path taken by the Outcast's blade. It has closed enough that the bleeding has ceased, but the skin still looks irritated.

"Why hasn't it fully healed?" I ask, noticing Shadow's frown.

"Because it's not life-threatening," Shadow answers. "You might want to ask Sara to pray over it or ask the Lady or the One yourself."

I'm not sure why his answer surprises me, but I'd never considered his beliefs before.

Will this wound heal completely?

I'm not sure whom I'm addressing, but the answer comes from the Lady.

"The blade that struck you is called 'Dimi,' which means 'destruction' or 'loss.' It carries a powerful poison meant to destroy the victim from inside," she explains. *"I have healed what I can for now, but your body will need time to fight the rest of the poison. Do not fear for your life in this, but know that until the poison passes or is driven away, there will be lingering pain. Fight despair with the knowledge of what you've purchased with your sacrifice."*

My tired mind is slow to pick up on her meaning.

"Watch over the boy."

With Uncle Jack gone, Alec has become our responsibility—my responsibility.

"Do you have your answer?" asks Shadow.

"I do," I reply. "It's something I'm going to have to work through."

"Right, then hold still while I fix this dress," says Shadow. Once again using Tellen's dagger, Shadow cuts off a large swath of cloth from the bottom of the dress and fashions a new sash. I think he's going to resort to crudely tying it in place, but to my pleasant surprise, he conjures a needle and dark thread from the Veil and stitches it in place. Satisfied with his handiwork, Shadow returns Tellen's dagger.

"What's going to happen to me?" Alec directs the question to me with his eyes.

Despite sharp pain in my side, I struggle to a sitting position. Tellen and Shadow help by turning me to face Alec. He's leaning against Katrina.

"You can come with us," I offer.

Katrina looks concerned.

"Vic, we're likely headed into a war zone," she says. "We should leave him in Caramore. He'll be safe there amongst our people."

"*We* might not be safe amongst your people," Tellen reminds her, pointing to Shadow and himself.

Although it's said lightly, there's weighty truth to his words. I feel the futility of our task pressing down on me.

"Despair can never have what you do not give it."

The One's voice speaks the words into my mind and soul. It will probably take me months to absorb the full meaning of the statement, but I understand it to be encouragement and let it minister to my sinking spirits.

"We need to go to the temple." I can feel solid truth in the words even before they leave my lips. "People are dying."

"Can you open a portal in your condition?" Shadow asks.

"I'm not dead yet," I assure him.

"Where are we going?" Alec sounds excited.

"The Alamon Temple," Katrina answers.

"Why are we going there?" Alec wonders.

We're going to have to get used to questions if we keep company with this boy. We exchange glances, questioning how much to reveal.

"There's a large battle happening there," I say at last. "We're going to end it."

"How are you going to do that?" Alec asks.

How indeed? I wonder silently. I do not receive an answer this time, but I'm not concerned yet.

"Hush, now," says Katrina. "I will explain more if there's time later."

Tellen and Shadow lift me to my feet and support my arms as I work through finding the right portal link. Much like finding Fort Medron, it takes me several tries before the Alamon Temple appears in the portal's preview.

The sight of it hits me hard. Parts of the temple are on fire. Bodies lay across the path leading up to the front gate, which has been sealed with large timbers. The battle continues despite the late hour, but the enemy is currently regrouping for a final push. Men, women, and even children stand along the wall holding anything that could be a weapon. They look exhausted.

I have no wish for Alec to be exposed to danger, but I can't leave him here alone either.

"Katrina, I'm going to open two portals," I say. "Take Alec to Caramore."

"We're going with you," she declares, shaking her head.

"Why?" I can't keep the pain out of my voice. "There's nothing there to find but destruction and death."

She points to the portal's image.

"That is our fate if we fail here," Katrina points out. "If we let that continue, both sides will call for war, and the only winner will be the Dark Man."

"At least put him somewhere safe before joining us out front," says Tellen. His expression tells me he understands her need to be present.

Shadow hasn't voiced an opinion, and when I look at him, I can tell his mind's not quite with us. My friend's face mask cannot hide the concern in his eyes.

"What are you thinking?" I ask him.

"We need to find my father and sister," Shadow says grimly. "They are there, which means the Resolute are seeking a way into Caramore. If an invasion happens, the Tariku League will have to declare war."

"How can you tell your father and sister are there?" Katrina asks.

Shadow points to a body in the lower left corner of the portal. The man's tunic is bright yellow and green.

"Those are the colors of the Pirok Guard. They only answer to the Supreme Huntmaster," Shadow explains. "If we can reason with him, maybe we can turn back the forces he's gathered by removing the legitimacy of the attack." He bows his head and studies the sand. "And if we can't reason with him, we can at least face him directly."

I don't want to think about having to fight the Supreme Huntmaster. Shadow's father, Jordan Lekros, might stand on the opposite side, but that doesn't mean we wish him dead. I'm convinced now that he's deceived not evil. I don't know when or how I drew that conclusion, but I believe he can be redeemed.

"I'm still going to open two portals, one inside the temple for Katrina and Alec to step through, and one outside the temple wherever the Supreme Huntmaster has pitched his tent," I say. "Tellen, Shadow, and I will speak with him. Katrina, find every Minder you can. Try to get reinforcements from Caramore. We're going to need them regardless of our chat with the Supreme Huntmaster. The undead are not going to negotiate, and I have serious doubts about the rest of the Resolute surrendering."

Chapter 23:
Dina's Deal

The Lady
Supreme Huntmaster's Camp, Tranquil Plains near the Alamon Temple

The guards on duty outside the Supreme Huntmaster's tent snap to attention when Victoria, Tellen, and Shadow step through the portal that materializes in the center of the camp. One guard casts a shield over the entrance while the other draws his sword and moves to block their path.

"I need to see my father," Shadow says. He holds both hands up to show he's not a threat.

"Have you come to join us, Shadow?" asks the guard who had stepped forward. He forms a ball of energy and casts it into the sky above the party, lending light to the area. "We would welcome you home if you had."

A silent alarm must have spread throughout the camp because huntsmen slip out of their tents and gather around the portal. Tellen keeps his hands near his daggers but does not draw them. Victoria stays behind her protectors and bids the portal to stay in case they need to exit quickly. I do not believe the Supreme Huntmaster would have Victoria killed, but he might try to capture her for his new master.

"No. I've come to save you from making a grave mistake," Shadow replies.

The shield the first guard placed over the tent entrance disappears in a flash and three figures leave the tent. The first is a beautiful young woman with brown hair and blue eyes. She wears a white blouse with short sleeves and a dark blue skirt. Her shoulders, waist, and

121

wrists are covered with thin gold plates that serve as adornment and armor. She holds a spent scroll in her hands. I know the conjuring scroll bound two Denkari for those are the two beings who step out behind her.

Both Denkari are tall and handsome with clean-shaven, pale faces and shaggy blond hair. They wear light green pants with a white tunic over top. White, red, and gold threads are woven together to make their outer robes. A gold sash sweeps downward across their chests from left to right. Each carries a heavy ceremonial staff with a retractable blade at the top. In unison, the spirit blades slide out of the top and snap into place with faint clicks.

The crowd of normal huntsmen stiffens.

"Welcome home, Devin." The young woman opens a small hole in the Veil and tucks the used scroll inside before resealing the breach.

"Dina. What have you done?" Shadow barely gets the question out. His eyes take in the Denkari flanking his sister.

Dina disappears from where she was standing and reappears behind Tellen. He leaps away and whirls, keeping a careful eye on Dina and the Denkari.

"Shadow, you should move," Tellen warns.

Shadow doesn't seem to hear him. He stands rooted in place.

Dina approaches with the slow grace of a hunting panther.

"I made a deal, dear brother," says Dina with a small smile. "Join us and they get to live."

As she finishes speaking, the Denkari direct their attention to the crowd, unleashing an intense mental assault that drives everybody to their knees. A few have the strength to moan, and some lean on staffs to keep their heads up. The Denkari reach mental tendrils toward Vic's party, but because I'm protecting them, the tendrils slip off without affecting them.

Victoria's bracers are in their defensive form, but she makes no move to intervene. She understands that Shadow needs to handle this. A stream of silent prayers flows out of her.

"What have you done to Father?" asks Shadow.

Dina waves toward the tent she'd come out of earlier.

"He's resting. When he awakens, he'll have a slight headache then be fine. He and I had a … disagreement about our role in this contest."

Shadow reaches up and removes his mask before asking another question.

"What sort of disagreement?"

"He wasn't happy about our allies," Dina explains.

"The Darkland creatures," Tellen supplies.

She confirms it with a nod.

"They're only here to help us claim what's rightfully ours," says Dina. "Think of them as being on loan from a benevolent master."

"There's nothing benevolent about him," Victoria mutters.

Dina regards Victoria a few seconds before her eyes brighten with new knowledge. She must be in close contact with the Outcast, but thankfully, I do not feel his presence here.

"I see you keep esteemed company, Devin," Dina notes. She offers Victoria a half-bow. "Welcome, favored one of the Lady. My master tells me it's been a long day for you and your companions. You should rest and eat." She shakes her head sympathetically and points to Victoria's side. "You're in no condition to be fighting other people's wars."

Victoria clutches her side where the dagger wound has started bleeding again. The Outcast must have reached her through the poison that coated the dagger. I don't think the connection's strong enough to allow him to truly harm her, but any connection is worrisome.

"I trust that I'll have the strength I need when I need it," Victoria states. Despite the words, her breaths grow labored and sweat breaks out on her brow as her magic bracers battle the poison.

"Your faith will get you killed," Dina declares. She sighs dramatically. "But I see that such a day is not meant to be this day. Pity. You would make a great ally. My master only wishes to help us liberate this world from the apathy that has gripped it for centuries."

"Dina, please," begs Shadow. "Listen to us, the Outcast promises much, but he lies! He's not here to help. He wants to conquer."

Dina's eyes become unfocused.

"The dead will have rest when this is over," she says.

"Yes," Shadow agrees, "but not by serving the Outcast. He's the one who enslaves them."

"Last chance to join the strong," Dina offers, eyes locked on her brother. "The Resolute await a strong leader. You could be that, brother."

"They won't follow you," says Shadow.

"They won't know it's me," Dina retorts with a grin. "Anybody can wear a mask and disguise their voice. You taught me that much." She proves it by rendering the next words with a deep enough pitch to pass for a young man. "The time has come for the Arkonai to reclaim Aeris." Turning to the Denkari, she returns to a normal voice. "Test the huntsmen. Gather the ones who wish to join the cause and kill the rest."

"Leave if you must, but everybody is free to choose their side," says Victoria. She waves to the portal behind her, straightens, and raises her voice. "This portal will let you join the defenders of the Alamon Temple. Serve the Outcast or serve the One. There is no longer an in between."

With my aid, Victoria breaks the mental shackles the Denkari placed on the huntsmen. Slowly, they rise and align themselves with Victoria or with Dina. A little more than half the huntsmen take their places behind Dina. The sides stare at each other grimly, awaiting the order to break the temporary truce.

"Go get my father," Dina orders her followers.

"No!" shouts Shadow.

"No," echoes Victoria, softer than her friend. "He too must be allowed to choose a side." She walks forward on slightly unsteady legs. Pausing a moment, she turns back to those who stand behind her. "Step through and prepare for battle. I will meet you at the temple later."

They salute Victoria by placing their right fists over their hearts and lowering their heads. Then, they start to file through the portal. One of the Denkari conjures a dozen spirit shards and flings them into the crowd. Victoria's bracers flash with white light and she sweeps the spirit shards off to the side, plowing them into a canvas sack of potatoes. Seeing she's distracted, the other Denkari levels his ceremonial staff at her, mentally detaches the blade, and hurls it at Victoria. Her bracers flare again. She spins and catches the blade in between her hands before letting it drop to the ground. It disappears upon landing, and a new blade forms atop the Denkari's staff.

The rest of the exodus takes place swiftly and peacefully.

When the last huntsman with a change of heart steps through the portal, Tellen goes to Victoria's side and takes one of her arms. Shadow falls into step on Victoria's other side, and together, they escort her through the huntsmen aligned with Dina. The crowd parts.

Stepping through the tent, they find that Dina has teleported to the Supreme Huntmaster's bedside ahead of them. Looking conflicted, she stands on the far side of the cot near the head with a dagger clutched in one hand.

"Please, don't make me kill him," she whispers, sounding genuinely afraid.

"To serve me, you must be willing to sacrifice anything." The Outcast's disembodied voice booms throughout the tent. "But bring him to me. I will measure his worth."

Relief floods Dina's features. She tucks the dagger into the sheath built into the gold belt wrapped around her waist. Placing both hands on the Supreme Huntmaster's sleeping form, Dina creates a portal and steps into the Veil, carrying her father with her on a wave of magic.

Shadow rushes to the empty cot.

When Dina reappears, he grabs one of her arms.

"Bring him back," Shadow pleads. Intense heat moves through the hand touching his sister's arm. Shadow cries out.

"My master will protect me," Dina says to Shadow. "That is but a small taste of what awaits those who defy him."

She teleports outside the tent again and sweeps her followers away.

Tellen ducks outside to witness the exit. Dina clasps hands with the two Denkari who raise their hands over the crowd of huntsmen as if to bless them.

Inside the tent, Shadow stares down at the empty bed in disbelief. Fear and sorrow battle within him.

Tellen returns. He and Victoria let Shadow grieve before offering any encouragement.

"We know he lives," Tellen declares.

"And we'll find him," Victoria adds.

I channel resolve into Shadow. Later, I will give him peace, but for now, the resolve will let him fight in the coming battle.

The Outcast will not move Jordan Lekros far, especially if he wishes to turn the man into a commander. Maybe I can send Adam after him, but I have another task for him. He has a presentation to make for Victoria's sake.

Chapter 24:
Mighty Defenders

Katrina Polani
Central Meeting Chamber, Alamon Temple

Alec Castaloni and I step through Vic's portal into the Central Meeting Chamber of the Alamon Temple. Because there has been a siege in place since the day before, the welcome we receive is hostile. Expecting this, I stay near the portal and keep Alec firmly behind me. Swords and spears point in our direction and several people shout for us to raise our hands and get on our knees. I obey and hope Alec has the sense to do the same.

A man wearing the red and gold armor of a temple guardsman pushes one of the swordsmen aside. His flowing cape tells me he's probably in charge.

"Who are you? What are you doing here? And why shouldn't my men kill you?" demands the man.

"We came with the Chosen Redeemer. We're here to save you," pipes up Alec. His youthful voice causes the men around us to laugh, scoff, or smile.

The commander's eyes drill into me, telling me he still wants an answer.

"My name is Katrina Polani," I say. "The boy behind me is Alec Castaloni. What he says is true: we're here to offer help."

"How do you intend to help?" asks the commander.

"May I lower my arms?" I wonder.

"Not until you answer the question," he says tightly.

"If you let me contact my father through a Minder, I will have him send reinforcements from Dominance," I explain. "I don't know

126

what's been decided in our absence, but I know at least some Saroth will come."

"I'm a Minder," says Alec. "I can help."

The commander eyes us both suspiciously.

"My name is Captain Gerard Rillis. You may lower your arms, but you'll have to let my men bind you until someone verifies your story."

"Bindings won't do much good on me. I'm a Shapeshifter, but I'm willing if you'll listen," I say, slowly lowering my arms. "May I stand?"

The captain's curt nod grants permission.

I rise and let two of the guards bind my wrists with thin metal shackles. I only protest when they move to do the same to Alec.

"Leave the boy. He's been through enough."

They look to their captain and receive a shrug, so they release Alec who steps close to me. The portal Vic sent us through disappears and we resign ourselves to waiting. Eventually, an old man approaches. He too wears shackles on his wrists, but they've gone further with him and bound his waist and his ankles. He can do little more than shuffle forward. The sight of his wild white hair and haunted gray eyes strikes me. When he's mere feet away, I finally recognize him.

"Master Patros," I whisper his name with shock and awe. This is one of the most respected Shapeshifter masters of our time. Anger causes my cheeks to flush, but I control it through great effort. "Why are you wearing chains?"

"Much the same reason you are, I think," replies the master. He looks to the captain and continues, "You believe in your heart that they'll come to their senses."

"Do you know this girl?" asks Captain Rillis.

Master Patros's eyes flick over to me.

"I've never met her, but she knows me," he answers. "Who does she claim to be?"

"A Shapeshifter by the name of Katrina Polani," supplies the captain.

"Ah." Master Patros focuses on me more carefully. "Well, I know the name, of course. Her father owns a lot of land near Jorash."

"Is she a Shapeshifter?" presses the captain.

"A skilled one, according to Arabeth Talini," Master Patros confirms.

"Have you seen her lately? Is she well?" I know I'm supposed to keep quiet until Captain Rillis makes a decision, but I can't help it. Mention of my master ignites a longing to know her fate. I've not seen her in several weeks.

"Last I heard from her was a month ago," says Master Patros. "She was traveling to Outreach to test a new apprentice candidate."

We chat quietly while the captain confers with the finely dressed people in the room. I gather they're part of the ruling council, but I don't know enough about the inner workings of the temple to predict their exact roles.

Finally, the captain allows me to instruct Alec to contact my father. I explain to Alec where he should cast his thoughts and what he should say once he makes a connection.

Soon, three figures appear in the room: my brother Adam, a Specter, and a Nokarti Assassin. Guardsmen stand at the ready, but since I warned them, they stop just shy of threatening the newcomers. Introductions ensue. The Specter—Dante Aurelius—is the same youth who helped Adam rescue Tellen and me on the Plains of Forgiveness. The Nokarti Assassin is Commander Jesella Creed. She reports that the Tariku League won't commit Caramore's armies, but they've also not forbidden individuals and companies from volunteering.

"My master requests that you release his daughter and Master Patros and let them help with the battle efforts," says Commander Creed. "I don't have firm numbers yet as we've only activated a few Specters."

I'm pretty sure there are only a few Specters, but I'm guessing that's not something Commander Creed wants widely known, even to potential allies.

Before the captain can respond, another portal appears and a few dozen huntsmen pour through. I sense the danger instantly. The portal means Vic sent them, but the temple guards don't know that. They're going to think it's an attack. Catching Master Patros's eye, I try to convey my fears in a glance.

Turning into a beetle, I slip out of the useless chains, fly to the portal, and turn back into my human form. Shouts rise up everywhere. The temple guards demand the huntsmen surrender and the latter prepare to defend themselves. Both groups brandish weapons and wait for somebody to make a move. I stand between them hoping to stop a bloody battle through sheer will.

Stop! Alec's thought rings with enough force to buy a moment's silence. He must have touched every mind at once.

"We are all on the same side," I say to Captain Rillis's men.

"These men tried to break down the temple gates just yesterday," one of the guards notes.

"We're here to join you," says one of the huntsmen. "The Chosen Redeemer showed us a better way. We will help you fight the Darkland creatures."

"I don't believe that for a second," murmurs another temple guard.

Many others agree with him. The tension stays until Tellen, Shadow, and Vic step through the same portal that the huntsmen came through. I explain the situation to my friends. We agree the Arkonai and Saroth defenders will need to be split up.

Since the Arkonai are best suited for fighting the Bereft and Resolute huntsmen, they're sent to the front of the temple. Tellen and Shadow accompany them since the huntsmen are comfortable taking orders from them. Commander Creed, Master Patros, Adam, Alec, and I go to the back to decide where to place the Saroth volunteers. It's not a perfect system, but at least the two halves of our help won't kill each other before the battle.

Throughout our inspection tour, Alec's been my faithful shadow. Eventually, I take him to the lower meditation room where the noncombatants have been housed.

"I want to stay with you!" he insists when he realizes my intent. He catches my hands and squeezes hard. "I want to fight!"

I kneel before the boy.

"There are many ways to fight, Alec," I begin. "You want to raise a sword against the enemy, but that is something any man can do. You can do something most men cannot."

"What's that?" he asks.

"You're a Minder. You can remind them why they fight," I explain. "Not every mind will be open to you, but search those that are, find what drives them, and give them hope. That will sustain them better than anything. If we lose hope, we are doomed."

His expression tells me he doesn't believe me. I'm at a loss for how to reach him when Dante appears by our sides with Sara Andari. The Specter disappears before I can thank him, but Sara quickly takes charge of young Alec. Since she seems to understand the situation already, I'm guessing the Lady forewarned her.

"Come help me organize this lot," Sara invites Alec. "We've much to do in scant time. The One and the Lady are with us, but ya can see the fear in the people's eyes. It's our job to drive it off, it is. Will ya help me?" She holds out a hand to him.

Alec drops my hands and takes Sara's hand. He looks at me uncertainly, but I can see he's smitten with her. I smile reassuringly and take my beetle form. It's easier to maneuver around this crowded temple by flying.

Midway back to the Central Meeting Chamber, a shudder runs through the whole temple. The attack has begun. I switch directions to go to the back entrance. Much of the Alamon Temple has been carved from the mountain itself, but there's a flat area beyond the back entrance with only a short wall separating it from the steep drop.

When I arrive, I see preparations are proceeding. A line of seven Conjurers have built the wall up to almost twice its original height. Two Minders bicker over a makeshift map on the ground. They make changes with thoughts, repositioning troops and arguing about where to find the weakest points of the battle line.

In beetle form, I fly high above the staging area to glimpse what comes our way. The sight is at once terrifying and beautiful. The two nearest peaks of the Black Horn Mountains are bleeding undead creatures. Most are zombies, but I count at least eight kitsarue and four Denkari. An angry black dragon flies over the horde, spewing purple tinged flames into the air.

I dive to the ground to find Vic, but she's standing in the center of the swirling activity with arms crossed, calmly watching the dragon bluster. I marvel at how much has changed in my young friend. Fair or not, she's had to grow up a great deal in the last few weeks. Landing next to her, I give her a questioning look.

"How are you this calm?" I ask. "Doesn't the dragon worry you?"

"Not today," Vic replies.

Dante appears next to Vic.

"Are you ready?" he asks her. "They've finally agreed on the perfect spot for you."

"I am," says Vic.

"Can I come?" I ask.

I know her answer before she shakes her head.

"Not this time. Wait, watch, and pray." With that pithy statement still sinking in for me, Vic disappears with the Specter.

Wanting the greater mobility, I switch to beetle form and once again rush headlong into the sky. At first, I see nothing new, but then,

Vic appears in the center of the main path leading to the back gate. The undead, kitsarue, Denkari, and other Darkland creatures sprint forward.

Light flashes out of her bracers, consuming most of the arrows flying her way. She catches the remaining projectiles and hurls them back at their sources. Vic seems to be everywhere. It's like she's a Specter in her own right, appearing and disappearing at will. Several terrifying times, I lose track of her.

After she softens the enemy, Vic is joined by Commander Jesella Creed and a dozen Nokarti Assassins. Undead creatures turn to dust by the hundreds. Two of the assassins fall, one to a Denkari's spirit shard and another to a random arrow. Their losses tug at my heart, but I continue to watch. I almost dive down and join the fray, but the rest of Vic's instructions play out in my mind. Instead, I fumble through a prayer for protection instead.

Four Denkari move in on Vic, but Dante appears and pulls her to a new location before they can truly trap her. The dragon roars in rage and sets six trees on fire around Vic and Dante. Vic leans over to speak to the Specter, and Dante disappears. He reappears below me looking unhappy, but he jogs over to the Minders monitoring the battle to await further instructions.

Meanwhile, Vic has moved to a clearing in the valley and faces off against the dragon. For a time, the dragon spits fireballs at her, but he stops once he realizes she can dodge them too well. Frustrated, he turns on the party of Nokarti Assassins, but Vic reclaims his attention by darting in and stabbing the dragon in the foot. He roars again and retreats into the sky.

Diving down, the dragon flattens Vic with the wind from his wings and pins her under the foot she stabbed.

Just when I think Vic will die, Adam springs out of a crowd of zombies in his wolf form. Diving forward, he initiates the change to human form. It's slower than my change, but he completes it before reaching the dragon and thrusts a dagger into the same foot that Vic wounded.

Light from Vic's bracers consumes them all.

Seconds later, the dragon flies off, turning the tide of the battle.

The zombies continue to fight on, but I know it's over with the dragon gone. Somehow, I'm certain that's not the last we've seen of the dragon, but for now, Vic and Adam have won the day.

Chapter 25:
Three Chosen Ones

Victoria Saveron
Central Meeting Chamber, Alamon Temple
The battle for the Alamon Temple lasts many hours. Dante Aurelius and I work hard to move troops. The two Minders that came with the Saroth—Erin Relco and Morgan Fazio—argue like crazy, but they manage to coordinate the Nokarti Assassins. As frontline fighters, the assassins take the most casualties of the Saroth, but they also turn hundreds of zombies into dust every few minutes. On the other side of the temple, the small band of recruited huntsmen fights the Resolute Arkonai and the Bereft soldiers. Even with guns, the Bereft are no match for the huntsmen.

The Lady's presence hovers above the battlefield and ministers to the wounded and dying on both sides. She wants to end the fighting but knows that the hatred has festered too long. I don't often sense her feelings, but since the fighting started, I've opened my emotions to her more than usual.

The Outcast has planned this war for a long time. Like it or not, I will have to see it through until the end. The thought of the war hurts the Lady, but she rejoices that truths will become clearer now. Peace has led many into spiritual apathy. People will have to choose a master now: the One or the Outcast.

When Galeric and the Resolute Arkonai retreat, the Bereft soldiers also surrender. Several huntsmen guard the Bereft prisoners while the rest head to the back to continue the fight against the undead. Finally, the Denkari and kitsarue retreat into the Veil, leaving the last few zombies to fight alone. The Nokarti Assassins make short work of them.

My friends and I meet with the council and representatives from both groups of defenders in the Central Meeting Chamber to discuss our tentative alliance. The Minders allow us to speak directly with the Tariku League and the Arkonai High Council. Both eventually acknowledge the need to pursue peace, yet there's sharp disagreement over where and when to formally meet.

Tellen and Shadow struggle to reason with their fellow Arkonai, and Katrina does the same with the Saroth, but it's been a long night and tempers are short. We won't solve the deep-seated issues between the Arkonai and the Saroth tonight. When nothing much gets accomplished in two hours, the Council sends both envoys back to their camps and sets up a meeting for later in the afternoon.

The Keeper of Knowledge, Master Ori, asks Adam and me to stay behind. Katrina, Tellen, and Shadow express wishes to stay. He nods permission and waits for everybody else to leave.

"Should Sara be present?" I wonder.

Having met Sara during the siege, Master Ori agrees and sends a scribe to fetch Sara Andari from below. The slight delay allows us to eat and rest. Master Ori spends the minutes checking scrolls, pacing, and muttering to himself.

"I apologize for making ya wait," says Sara upon entering the room. "Do ya mind if the lad comes in as well? He oughtn't be alone just now."

"I think this is a message for everyone to hear," Master Ori replies. "If he's content to listen, then he's welcome."

Sara whispers instructions to Alec and ushers him in. He and the scribe exchange excited smiles and bound into the room. Sara herds them over to where we're seated on cushions. Etienne picks up the materials to record the conversation, but Master Ori stops him.

"Do not work right now, Etienne," says Master Ori. "You are here to be a witness, not a scribe. There will be time to record these proceedings later. For now, simply rejoice. We are greatly blessed by the presence of two of the three Chosen Ones today."

His announcement confuses nearly everybody. Adam gives a small, almost imperceptible smile. I frown thoughtfully. Tellen and Shadow exchange puzzled glances. The boys start to ask questions, but Sara hushes them. Katrina is the first to understand Master Ori's meaning.

"Vic and Adam," she says, staring hard at her twin brother. "But how can that be?"

"The One and the Lady choose whom they will," Sara notes with a shrug. "Tis the way life has always been and always will be."

Beaming at Sara, Master Ori directs his next question to her.

"Do you know why there are three Chosen Ones, young lady?"

"Aye. They represent the three forms of the One: spirit, body, and mind," Sara explains. "His Chosen One is called the Favored Son. The Lady's grace rests upon the Chosen Redeemer, and the third was selected by the Spirit of Truth. He or she will be called the Sage."

"Well said," praises Master Ori. "I believe we have now met the Son and the Chosen Redeemer." He waves for Adam and me to come close and waits until we do so. Then, he picks up Adam's left hand and my right hand and brings the two together. "You are stronger together, but you must find the Sage to reach your full potential as Redeemers. Only then will you be able to deliver the world from the Outcast and his servants."

"How will we find the Sage?" I ask. Adam's hand is warm and comforting, so I let my hand linger a few more heartbeats before retrieving it.

"I don't know for sure," Master Ori admits, "but I may be able to offer you clues from the books and scrolls. For example, you should probably look amongst the Arkonai in remote places, perhaps even someone raised by Bereft. I can be more specific if you give me a little time with the primary sources."

Calling Etienne and Alec over, Master Ori rattles off a long list of titles for the boys to fetch from the library. He waits until they're gone before continuing. "Such a journey should be undertaken soon, but it will be very dangerous. The Outcast knows that the Favored Son and the Chosen Redeemer are active."

"I know he knows about me," I say, "but how does he know about Adam?"

"The dragon you fought earlier is called Malcorius," says Master Ori. "He and his kin have long served the Outcast. I'm sure he has already given a full report on the matter."

"Lots of people fight dragons," I argue. "That alone shouldn't be a declaration of his identity."

"There's a prophecy," Adam says with another smile.

I should have known that. Seems there's a prophecy about everything. If I had more time, I'd stop and study them. Maybe it'd give me good directions about what to do with my life, assuming I survive the next few years.

"The Outcast will do anything to stop you from finding the third Chosen One. I don't think you should take the young boy with you." Master Ori looks troubled.

"What will happen to the lad?" asks Sara.

"I can see if my father will make him an apprentice," Katrina offers. "He is a Minder after all, as is Alec. He has potential, but he'll need proper training." She frowns. "I just hope Lady Corabelle doesn't take an interest in him. He is her grandson. That gives her a strong claim to his care."

I suppress a shudder at the mention of my grandmother. My encounter with her in Dominance wasn't exactly what I'd imagined meeting my mother's mother would be. If that's what my mother had to deal with growing up, it's not very surprising that she ran away to the farthest Bereft village she could find. Thoughts of Grandmother brings up thoughts of Uncle Jack. I'm not sure whether to fear what the Outcast will do to him or fear what he'll do for the Outcast.

"Who should go on the journey?" Sara's question pulls me from thoughts of Uncle Jack. Her eyes take in each of us in turn.

"Just us," I answer, looking to Adam. My throat turns dry and painful. I don't want to leave my friends, but there's a part of what's to come where they cannot follow.

"Vic, you can't protect us by avoiding us," Katrina says patiently. "We heard the Outcast's threat, and I for one don't care. He hates us because of whom we serve."

I attempt a smile for her. Impressions from the Lady fill me, giving me insight into each of my friends.

"It's not that this time," I say, struggling to share my feelings. My left side hurts where I got stabbed. I have to resist the urge to clutch it. If I show any weakness, they'll never agree to do what needs to be done. "You and Tellen are probably the only ones who can hold any alliance between the Arkonai and the Saroth together. Adam and I will try to stop the Darkland creatures from finding their way here, but you'll have to deal with what's already broken through. Shadow wants to find his father and his sister, and Sara's at home in the temple."

"Home is with ye for the moment," says Sara.

"I can find my father and sister with you," Shadow argues. "You promised to help me."

"I will keep that promise, but we may go places you cannot enter." I say the words to Shadow, but I mean them for all of my friends.

Sorrow hits me, and I've never been so alone amongst people I love.

"Let us go with you until we reach that point," says Tellen.

"If we bring a Specter with us, we can return to safety when the time is right," Katrina reasons. "I might be able to convince my father to let Dante come with us."

"I can port you to safety if necessary," I point out. "That's not the problem."

"Then what is?" Katrina snaps.

"We can't bring light everywhere if we huddle together," I say, silently thanking the Lady for the image that prompted the words. "We must spread out and each do our part. Adam and I will find the third Chosen One. I can't tell you what you should do. I can only identify what you're good at."

Tears pool in her green eyes.

"What will I do without you?" Katrina asks.

I pick up her hands and meet her discouraged gaze.

"You're a peacekeeper. You will fight hard to unite the Arkonai and the Saroth," I answer. "And I'm not going away just yet. It will take time to figure out where we should go and how we should get there." I wave to the temple around us. "This is a good place to rest and think."

One by one, I share with them the thoughts the Lady has been pouring into me over the last few minutes. Master Ori has always delighted in learning. He will be a good mentor for Sara if she wants to stay, but she's worried about her parents in Coldhaven. I offer to take her home to check on them. If she wants to bring them back to the temple, I'm sure those arrangements can be made. If Master Ori can't handle them, Keeper Jemma Heston can help.

In his father's absence, Shadow inherits the responsibilities of the Supreme Huntmaster until a new one can be elected. He can either return to Bastion to lend stability to the Arkonai High Council or he can pursue his father and sister. Both are things that need to happen, and we will need a representative to carry our wishes to that council anyway. They will never fully trust my father.

Tellen and Katrina are ideal for being the buffer between the combat forces of the Arkonai and Saroth. Both peoples will be needed to protect the Bereft from the Darkland invaders. A war between the Arkonai and Saroth is still possible, but it is less likely now that they are aware of the Outcast's plan to sow discord. The friendship that started between my friends on our trek to Coldhaven has become deeper and stronger. It saddens me that they must hide their feelings from their people in the interest of maintaining peace. Prejudice runs too deep to let love flourish openly right now. I don't say this because they already know it, and if the others have not figured it out by now, it's none of their business.

"It's not yet time to part ways," I say when I finish describing roles. "Let's sleep, help with the cleanup, and find a good game of darts to play. It's been a long time since I let Tellen beat me at that."

"There's no 'letting' about it. You're just terrible at darts," Tellen declares. He frowns thoughtfully. "Or at least you were. There's no telling what you'll be now."

"There's only one way to find out," I say.

THE END

Thank You for Reading:

Each book is a labor of love that I enjoy sharing with people. Don't miss the exciting conclusion of the Redeemer Chronicles trilogy. If you want to know what went on before Redeemer Chronicles starts, check out Aeris Legends.

Please visit my website: **www.juliecgilbert.com** to find a link to the current free works. It's my goal to set individual ebooks free, but if you still wish to show support, there are combination books and other formats to purchase. The audiobooks have fantastic narrators, and there is something special about paperbacks.

Join the Facebook group "Julie C. Gilbert's Special Agents" for monthly book discussions and giveaways.

I would love to connect via email: **devyaschildren@gmail.com**

Sincerely,

Julie C. Gilbert

www.ingramcontent.com/pod-product-compliance
Lightning Source LLC
Chambersburg PA
CBHW051250170626
46809CB00004B/1578